THE DRAGON'S PSYCHIC

IMMORTAL DRAGON, BOOK 1

LINZI BAXTER

LINZI BAXTER

CONTENTS

The Dragon's Psychic
Immortal Dragon, Book 1
Copyright © 2019 by Linzi Baxter
Cover Artist: Cassy Roop, Pink Ink Designs
Cover Model: Zack
Cover Photographer: Wander Aguiar
Edited by: Red Adept Editing

BLURB

Talia hadn't planned on dying today. Accidentally defying the supernatural council wasn't exactly her plan either. But when she did her duty and touched a bloody knife to determine guilt or innocence, her vision seemed... off. So was Councilman Gideon's rush to declare a shivering child guilty of murder. Now Talia's trying to lose herself in the West Virginia mountains with the child in tow, and the mercenary on their tail has an uncanny ability to find them, no matter how far they run.

Kirin's dragon-shifter senses make him the most sought-after mercenary in these parts. But something about this job smells wrong. And when he finally lays his hands on the fugitive, he gets the surprise of his three-hundred-year life. The fragile, determined woman in his arms is his mate, who he'd given up all hope of finding.

His mercenary target has become his chosen partner, and instead of breathing down her neck, he's bound to protect her at all costs. But if Kirin and Talia can't figure out who wants this child dead—and why—they could all wind up sharing the same grave.

AUTHOR NOTE'S

White Hat Security Series

Hacker Exposed

Royal Hacker

Misunderstood Hacker

Undercover Hacker

Hacker Revelation

Hacker Christmas

Hacker Salvation

Nova Satellite Security Series
(White Hat Security Spin Off)

Pursuing Phoenix - Sept 3, 2019

Immortal Dragon

The Dragon's Psychic - July 9, 2019

The Dragon's Human - Sept 26, 2019

Montana Gold (Brotherhood Kindle World)

Grayson's Angel

Noah's Love

Bryson's Treasure - 2019

A Flipping Love Story (Badge of Honor World)

Unlocking Dreams

Unlocking Hope - 2019

Siblings of the Underworld

Hell's Key

Hell's Future - Aug 20, 2019

Visit linzibaxter.com for more information and release dates.
Join Linzi Baxter Newsletter at Newsletter

1

TALIA

When the universe throws you a curve ball, you can either fight it head-on or run for your life.

The fresh air of the West Virginia mountains did nothing to calm Talia's nerves. It wasn't the first time the supernatural council had summoned her. Once the council found out about her ability, they used her to help solve cases, and now they called at least once a month. But something about that day's call made her uneasy.

If Talia could hide from the council, she would. Yes, she loved the money she made—it helped support her Jimmy Choo habit and kept a roof over her head. But the visions took a toll on her with each new case. It wasn't as if she could unsee her visions. The images haunted her in her dreams.

Each state had its own governing council. A handful of high-ranking government officials in each state's council governed the supernatural community. Only a few humans were aware of the supernatural world, and the supernatural beings wanted it kept that way. The council's headquarters for West Virginia were in the mountains, a few miles from Haven Springs, a small town inhabited mostly by shifters.

Talia had not only helped the West Virginia Council—sometimes other state councils also called when they needed her help. The council was made up of supernatural beings who had been around for centuries, whose moral compass only consisted of black-and-white beliefs.

Talia parked her red Toyota Corolla at the end of the gravel parking lot. She shifted in her seat and stared at the building, which resembled a warehouse. The morning sun hadn't burned off the layer of fog surrounding it. From the outside, the building looked small, but she knew that under the structure was a maze of offices and research labs. A chill went through her as she thought about the research labs. She'd overheard horror stories over the years about the criminals being used as test subjects.

Ever since Gideon, from the high council, had called, she felt like something bad was about to take place. Talia couldn't call in sick—the council would send someone to her one-bedroom apartment and drag her to the warehouse. Few people had her ability, and some days, it seemed more like a curse than a gift. Today was one of those times she wished she had no abilities, because she had an inkling that once she walked into the building, her life would change.

The council had placed cameras around the warehouse—Gideon would be informed the second Talia arrived. Even if she wanted, she couldn't sit in her car much longer, or Gideon would send a goon out to grab her. Talia's best friend, Nyx, had called her when she was in the parking lot a few weeks earlier, and they'd been on the phone for five minutes before one of Gideon's men had shown up at her car window, ushering her inside.

She took in a deep breath of the mountain air before she exited her car. The gravel crunched under her high heels as she walked toward the side entrance. Gary stood outside. He had been the day guard for as long as she'd worked for the council.

The council used trolls for protection around the building because they were particularly loyal.

No matter how many times Talia came to the council, Gary would motion for her badge. This time, she held it up, and he scanned it with his phone then nodded when a green check mark appeared on the screen. She grabbed the cold metal door and pulled it. Gideon had told her to head to the interrogation rooms.

Talia stopped at the security desk. "Hi, Olinda. Is this new?"

Every time Talia walked past Olinda's desk, a new flashy trinket was sitting on it. Fairies loved to collect sparkly charmed objects.

Olinda's face lit up as she reached for her glittery gold miniature gnome. "Yes. Gary bought it for me." She blushed.

Talia held back a smile. She couldn't image the petite blond fairy with the muscular Gary. He didn't resemble a troll unless he shifted, but he was close to seven feet tall, and his muscles had muscles.

"That was nice of him." Talia shifted to her other foot. "You have any clue why Gideon called me?"

Olinda was in charge of the front desk for the council and heard all the latest gossip. She might be able to give Talia a hint about what she was about walk into.

Olinda's lips turned down. "I have no clue why he called you in, but Gideon is in a bad mood. Something happened, and he isn't happy about it."

Great. Now I have to deal with a thousand-year-old grouch. She couldn't remember the last time he'd been in a good mood, but if Olinda thought he was mad, well, their meeting would be bad.

"Okay. I'll head back."

Olinda reached in her pocket and threw gold glitter on her. Talia hated when Olinda doused her in glitter, but the fairy didn't understand, and Talia didn't want to upset her. Talia mumbled a thank-you and walked through the door to the left of the receptionist's desk.

She stepped into the back, where TVs lined the far wall of the warehouse. Each TV displayed the local news around the state and country. A team scrutinized the news and waited for someone to shift in public. Within minutes, the council would have someone on the scene, cleaning up the mess. The council members perceived it was important to keep their abilities a secret so humans wouldn't do research on them, but it didn't stop them from using the lab in the basement on their latest criminal.

Talia bypassed the group working and walked down a plain hall to the back of the warehouse. On her way, she passed the stairway that led downstairs. In her years of helping the council, she'd never set foot downstairs, and she didn't plan to ever go down there.

Outside the interrogation room stood another guard. Talia didn't remember his name, but she knew he was one of the council's top guards. He stood with his arms crossed and a scowl on his face. Talia's stomach turned with uneasiness again. Instead of opening the door to the room with the suspect, the guard nodded to the next door. Talia grasped the handle and pulled.

Over the years, Talia had sent many supernaturals to life in prison and few to their deaths. Two years before, she'd observed a father murdering his family because he wanted to start over. The screams of his daughter as he stabbed her had stuck with Talia. She shook off the thought of the evil man she'd helped put away forever.

"Kael," she muttered as she entered the room. Gideon had always annoyed her, and his powers vibrated around the room, but Kael's power seemed beyond anyone's thoughts. Some days, her fingers itched to touch him and find out what he really hid under his perfect blank face. Talia believed he worked hard to cover who he really was, unlike Gideon, who let his powers out constantly. She didn't understand how Gideon didn't see Kael's power.

"Talia, we need your help on a case." Kael gestured toward the two-way mirror. "The knife is the key to putting the girl away." A long serrated kitchen knife wrapped in a white linen cloth sat on the silver metal cart, but that wasn't what caught Talia's attention in the four-by-four-foot interrogation room. No, it was the little girl sitting there, all of eight years old. Tears streaked down the girl's face, but it was the vacancy in her eyes that made Talia want to help her. The young girl stared down at her hands until her head jerked up and her eyes focused directly in Talia's direction. There was no way the girl could be aware of her on the other side of the glass, but she looked as if she was asking for help with her eyes before she glanced down at her blood-covered hands.

"What does the girl have to do with this?" Talia asked. There was no way that young girl had done anything wrong.

Kael crossed his arms. "She used the knife to murder Jalil and Maya Meadows."

"I have never met Jalil or Maya Meadows. Who are they?"

"They're both members of the council. Alida"—he nodded to the girl—"is their only child."

She couldn't hold back the frown. "So I'm here to prove the young girl killed her parents?" *Why would the little girl kill her parents, and since both of her parents are gifted, why would she use a knife and not her powers?* The whole thing was strange. She couldn't understand how a eight-year-old girl could over-power two council members.

"We need you to confirm what we think happened, and then we can put her on trial."

"What did the girl say?" Talia asked.

"She hasn't spoken."

"Why do you think she killed her parents if she hasn't spoken?"

Kael crossed his arms over his chest. "You're not here to ask questions. We brought you in for one job."

"Don't snap at me. I will get you your answers. You said her name is Alida?"

"It doesn't matter. I only need you to get a read of the knife."

"If you only wanted me to read the knife, you

should have taken it out of the room." Talia didn't know how to keep her mouth shut sometimes.

Kael cocked his head. "Yes, Alida is her name. Now, do what we pay you for."

Overgrown hotheaded council members were one of the other reasons Talia hated her job. She turned on her heel and left the observation room. The overgrown bodyguard opened the door to the interrogation room. She couldn't wait to get a read on the knife and prove the asshole in the observation room wrong.

Talia shivered as she entered the interrogation room. Someone had cranked the AC to a freezing temperature. Talia glanced at the two-way mirror. She knew Kael was watching her every move, and she couldn't help but mumble, "Asshole." It didn't surprise Talia to see her breath in the cold room. Talia was pretty sure Kael would be mad if she interacted with the girl and didn't just read the knife. But if they'd only wanted Talia to touch the knife, they should have taken it out of the room.

The metal chair screeched against the cement floor as Talia pulled it back from the table. The little girl gazed up from her bloody hands. Her blond locks had fallen out of her ponytail. Tears continued to stream down her face, but it was the blank look that crushed Talia's heart.

"Hi, Alida. My name is Talia."

The little girl didn't look up from her hands. She had to be in shock.

Talia didn't understand why the council had left the poor girl in the same room as the knife. Blood streaked down the side, and it looked menacing. This was the part of the job she hated. Normally, the reward for the pain she endured was knowing she would put a scumbag away. The thought of this young girl going to jail for this crime made her stomach churn.

Talia was staring at the knife on the cart for a couple of minutes when a loud knock sounded on the mirror. She jumped at the noise, but the young girl continued to stare numbly at her hands. Talia moved her hands toward the knife. She hated this part. When she touched an object, she wasn't just an observer—she could feel the pain and emotions of everyone in the room. If the scene was too bad, the vision would drain her body of its energy, and she would need to lie down.

The council had a room for her. She'd only had to use it a few times. The last time was when a wolf went rogue and killed an entire pack. The pain she'd felt when he killed the women and kids was enough to knock her out for three days.

After taking a few deep breaths, Talia reached for the knife. Her fingers locked around the black handle. The thing was heavy for a kitchen knife. This handle was the spot that should tell her who the killer was, since he or she would have held the weapon.

Images of death and destruction assaulted Talia as she gripped the knife. The copper smell of blood choked her, but it wasn't the scent that made it hard to concentrate on the vision—emotions were extremely strong in the room. She arrived in what she assumed was the kitchen of the little girl. They were all in the room together... Jalil, Maya, and Alida. The anger and sadness were so strong they caused blurriness around the edges and somewhat in the center. Then she saw the little girl standing over her dead parents, holding the knife.

Talia glanced at Alida in the vision. The little girl stared into her eyes. "I didn't do it."

Talia had never before experienced anyone talking to her in a vision. This girl had powers beyond anyone's belief. There was no way she would have killed her parents with a knife. Talia could feel the little girl's powers vibrating through the room.

She strained to see around the blurriness of the vision, but all she could hear was the little girl sob, "I didn't do it." Talia didn't know if Alida's powers or the emotions in the room were affecting her vision. She closed her eyes for a second to focus. She needed to find something to prove the girl's innocence. When she looked to the side, she saw a black figure.

Something pulled her out of her vision, and her body was transported back to the room. Exhaustion overtook her, but she needed to fight through it. If she hadn't already been sitting on the chair, she would have collapsed to the ground. The vision had taken an extreme amount of energy, but being pulled out of it had caused her stomach to turn. She looked around the room to find Arrow standing next to her with the knife in his hand.

"Why did you pull me out?" she asked.

"Your eyes rolled back, and you chanted a language nobody had ever heard."

"You had no right to pull me out." If she'd had more energy, she would have stood and gone toe to toe with the overgrown enforcer. But Arrow would never admit he'd done something wrong. Talia took her eyes away from the enforcer and studied Alida.

"What are her powers?" she asked without taking her eyes off the little girl.

Arrow shook his head. "Her parents told the council she had no powers. Gideon can't sense any powers in her. It doesn't matter. She used the knife to kill her parents. Is that what you saw?"

Talia didn't know how to explain the vision. If she admitted the girl could talk to her during it, Alida might be put in further danger. This was the first time she wouldn't tell the council her true vision—and technically, she hadn't seen the little girl kill anyone.

"She didn't kill her parents."

"I find that hard to believe. When the enforcers showed up to the house, they found her with a knife over her parents."

"How was the council notified so quickly about the murder?"

Arrow shrugged. "Someone called in an anony-mous tip."

"You're telling me someone called in a tip, and the council sent someone, and they got there fast enough to find her"—Talia pointed to the girl at the table—"with a knife in her hands, standing over her parents. Are you even listening to yourself?"

"Well, then, tell us who to look for."

"I'm telling you she didn't do it. If you are so convinced she did it, why am I here?"

"The council has protocols, and we need to follow them. We need a living witness to tell us what happened so we can prosecute her."

Talia leaned her head back and closed her eyes. The council members did everything to cover their own asses. Maybe if Talia touched the knife again, she would get another vision.

This time, she would touch the knife where Alida had been holding it. Another section might give her a better vision of the true killer. Talia's instinct told her the girl was innocent. But when she reached for the knife in Arrow's hand, he stepped back and glared at her.

"Why do you need touch the knife again?"

Fuck. He is questioning my vision. She needed a reason to touch the knife a second time. Before she had time to answer, the door to the interrogation room slammed opened, and Gideon entered.

Gideon wore his long dark council robe and had his hands tucked in the sleeves, which made her incredibly wary. Talia had never disobeyed the council and always came running when they needed her, but since she'd received the call to come to the warehouse, everything had felt wrong. Her conscience wouldn't let her see an innocent child convicted of something she hadn't done. And if Talia went against the council, she would spend the rest of her life in jail down below, or they would kill her. She'd seen the council's ways.

"Talia, we need to talk," Gideon began in a low voice. She could tell he was struggling to control his anger. He didn't even try to hide his disapproval. She waited to hear the worst.

2

KIRIN

The hot water rained down on Kirin's body. He couldn't shake the dream from the night before, the same one that had plagued him for the last month. In it, a woman was calling out his name. She needed him. His dragon wanted out of his human body to find the woman. He had woken up a few times close to shifting.

Kirin leaned his head back and let the water run down his body. He wished he could make out the woman's face so he could hunt her down and find out why she haunted him at night. Knowing he couldn't figure out the dream in the shower, Kirin reluctantly turned it off.

His muscles ached. He'd spent entirely too long

on his bike the night before, chasing a warlock the council had branded a traitor. He thought everyone would be safer with the rogue wizard off the streets and in the council's hands. The work he performed took a toll on his body, but it sure was profitable. His dragon needed the money. All he'd wanted the night before when he got home was a good night's rest, but that woman had haunted him in his dreams. Now not only did his muscles ache, but he was exhausted from the sleepless night as well.

He grabbed a towel and wrapped it around his waist, catching a glimpse of the red mark on his side. The warlock had sent a piece of scrap metal in his direction, and he hadn't been able to dodge it in time. Kirin was glad he was on the job alone, or one of his brothers might have laughed at him for letting a warlock get a piece of him. His dragon had healed the wound, and the only thing left was the red mark.

A dark cup of coffee would improve his morning. Kirin missed the simplicity of the old days but loved the new innovations of the last three hundred years. The coffeepot was his favorite. He popped a pod in the Keurig and waited for the liquid gold to brew. The dragon purred at the rich scent of the dark roast. Man and beast needed their daily fix. His dragon was cranky on the inside. Not only did Kirin want to look for the woman from his dreams, but the dragon also itched to break free and find her.

The last time his dragon had been this close to the edge, he'd burned down a city in the morning. One hundred and fifteen years before, he'd woken to the cries of a young girl in his backyard. His dragon thought the thugs would hurt her. After he burned down most of the neighborhood, including his house, he found out they were practicing for a play in school. Rebuilding the town cost a few gold bars out of his hoard. The gold dragon felt the kids deserved what had happened for disturbing his sleep. The local witches had needed to come in and wipe the memories of the people in the neighborhood. Luckily, no one had videophones back then.

With coffee in hand, Kirin walked back toward the bedroom and caught a glimpse of his eyes in the dresser mirror. They glowed gold. The dragon was thinking about the time he'd burned down the neighborhood. He still was angry that Kirin had helped rebuild it.

Kirin looked around his master bedroom. The mansion he'd built on the side of the West Virginia mountain gave him the escape from humanity his dragon needed. As the last gold dragon shifter, he struggled to find a mate. He had no one to rush home to, not even a pet. Deep down, he wondered if he'd never decorated because he longed for his mate, but if he hadn't found her in the last three hundred years, who knew if she would ever come.

Kirin wasn't about to break the news to his mother that he'd stopped searching for a mate. Nothing was worse than a pissed-off female dragon. For the last two hundred years, she'd asked each time they talked if he'd found his mate yet. She wanted grandbabies and was sick of waiting. The last time he talked to his mom, she promised he would find his mate soon. The inner dragon perked up at his mom's comment, but the human side had scoffed.

Kirin didn't think he would ever find his mate, so he might as well do what he was good at: capturing bad guys and hoarding as much money as possible. After all, dragon shifters were immortal, and one could never have too much money. Being a gold dragon, he hoarded gold more than any other treasure. His dragon pressed in his mind to go to the hoard. The dragon loved to look at everything they had acquired over the years. But they had things to do that day even if the dragon wanted something else.

He dressed in a pair of jeans and a black polo shirt before pulling on his black leather boots. Kirin liked to dress reasonably nicely before he picked up his latest payoff, which came after the council processed the traitor. He didn't have a clue what the council did to the people he caught after he turned them over. Kirin lived on the fringe of society. If it weren't for his mom and his two brothers, Kia and Conley, he would have no one in his life. And he wasn't sure he minded that a bit.

Kirin exited the main house and entered his six-car garage. The house had everything he ever wanted. The white floors in the garage sparkled with specs of gold. He found ways to bring gold into every aspect of his house. It helped calm his dragon. In the first stall of the garage sat his custom Harley Fat Boy. Kirin loved to ride his motorcycle. It was the closest he could get to feeling like he was flying. He missed the days when he could fly around and not worry about being caught on a smartphone or in a photograph. There was a lot of paperwork when the council had to remove humans' memories, and he had to pay a fine. Kirin didn't like to part with his money, so he chose to ride his bike during the day and let his dragon out late at night.

After Kirin slipped on his gloves and his

sunglasses, he drove to the new diner that had opened up on the way to the warehouse that hid the supernatural council's offices. He parked his bike in front. Even though the diner had opened a month before, it needed a fresh coat of paint and a new sign. The building had sat empty after the previous diner closed eleven years before. The new owners hadn't put any work into the outside and hadn't done much on the inside either, but the food was mouthwatering.

A rusty bell rang over his head as he opened the door to the diner and took a seat in the booth near the window on the far side of the building. It had become second nature to map out a room the second he walked in. The booth was near an emergency exit, and he could watch the front of the diner from there. The aroma of bacon and eggs filled the air.

He barely glanced at the middle-aged waitress as she took his order. His thoughts were on the coffee she poured. Kirin was tired from the night before and hoped the second cup of coffee would kick his ass in gear. The council had sent him on a different case each day for the past week, and it was time for a few days off. Kirin planned to collect his paycheck and spend a few days as his dragon.

He downed a dozen-egg omelet and three servings of bacon with an additional four coffees before he paid for his breakfast. Kirin wore his sunglasses the entire time because it was easier when dealing with humans. Still, the minute he gazed over the rim of his glasses to see better while he pulled out his cash, the waitress commented.

"What interesting eyes you have. What is that shade? Not exactly hazel. Kinda… golden brown, emphasis on the gold."

He nodded, gave her a healthy tip, and exited the diner. When he looked back before he got on the bike, he noticed the old lady's eyes turned in his direction.

Kirin had just started his bike when his phone vibrated. He sighed. It was his younger brother, Kia.

"What's up?" he asked gruffly.

"Just making sure you didn't forget that we're celebrating Conley's birthday tomorrow."

Kirin groaned. "He's two hundred thirty-four. It's not like it's his twenty-first or hundredth birthday. Hell, he's not even two hundred fifty. So why do we have to make a big deal out of it every year?"

Kia snickered. "Because he's the baby. I'm the middle forgotten dragon. And you're the big-brother dragon who flies under the façade of being a badass but is really a bunny inside."

"I'll make you regret those words," he teased. "Don't make me burn you, little brother. I know where you live."

"Coulda fooled me. You could fly here in twenty minutes, but I haven't seen you in six months. Since the Fourth of July, actually."

Kia wasn't one to mince words. It wasn't that Kirin didn't want to see his brother, but when he finally got time off work, he wanted nothing more than to relax in his house.

"I've been busy with work."

Kirin could almost see Kia roll his eyes. "You mean being Gideon's lapdog."

"I'm helping protect our kind and keeping the humans from finding out about us."

"Really? Have you ever stopped and asked what the person did before you brought them in? You don't have to answer that question. I know the answer. Just because Gideon is the head of the West Virginia Council doesn't mean you should do what he says without looking into his request."

He gripped the handles of his bike, needing somewhere to direct his anger. His younger brother had a point, but it didn't mean he had to constantly drag up the same argument. "Have you found something I should know about?"

Kia was a tech genius, and Kirin had no doubt he'd spent many hours hacking. Kirin worried every so often whether the council would tell him to bring his brother in. That would be the day Kirin would stop doing what the council wanted. His family was off-limits, and he would do anything to protect them. Maybe Kia was right when he'd called him a bunny rabbit.

"Nothing concrete yet, but something seems off. If you would ask more questions instead of only collecting your check, I might have something to go on."

A dull throb ached between Kirin's eyes. "I will keep an eye open." If he asked more questions, Gideon would catch on quickly. Nobody reached a thousand years old without being skeptical about everyone. And even if Kirin did get the info, he would put his brother in danger as he researched the council.

"The last person you brought in didn't get a trial. They executed him last night. Doesn't that feel off to you?"

"How the fuck do you know that? I was about to head in and see if the council had processed him. I will say one thing—he was a hard motherfucker to take down. If I had a say, I would execute him. Fucker took a chunk out of my side."

Kia let out a sigh. "Of course he was. The guy you brought in was a council member from Virginia. Do you understand what will happen when their council finds out who took him in?"

"Why didn't he say anything? He fought me from the second I found him." The dull pain had turned into a full-blown headache. Kirin would need to look over his shoulder constantly for the next few weeks.

"Do you ever stop and ask questions, or do you just try to take the person down so you can collect your money? Kirin, you used to question your assignments in the past, but now you go and do what Gideon says blindly for the money and try to finish as fast as you can."

"Fine. I will ask more questions. But you'd better stop hacking the council."

Kia laughed on the other end. "I don't know what you're talking about. But I have to go. Don't forget about Conley's birthday. Mom's coming. We will talk more." Their mom lived on an island off of Hawaii, and she didn't make it back very often.

When Kirin looked up, the waitress from earlier was staring at him through the dust-covered windows. Not paying her any more attention, Kirin started his Harley and let the vibration flow through his body. As he rode through the winding roads of West Virginia to the office, the conversation played back in his mind and left a bad taste in his mouth, but he pretended the problem was the subpar coffee.

3

TALIA

Talia stepped back when Gideon burst through the door. She wanted to be anywhere except that cold room. Over the years, Talia had come to learn that Gideon had a short fuse. That day was no exception. When he entered the room, his powers made the air thick and hard to breath. With a menacing step, he walked toward her, nostrils flared and jaw clenched. A chill ran down Talia's back. She'd seen Gideon angry before, but that had been nothing compared to his current state. She needed to put her big-girl pants on and go head-to-head with the High Council leader if she planned to help the girl.

With each passing second, the air became heavier, and Gideon's eyes turned from deep brown to black. She didn't understand how he knew she'd lied... well, stretched the truth. Arrow had rushed out the door the moment Gideon entered. For being the council enforcer, he'd left the room fast. *If Alida is so dangerous, why would the enforcer leave me alone with her and the head of the council?*

She waited for Gideon to speak first, hoping he would explain what she'd done to anger him, but he continued to glare at her with his black eyes.

"Hello, Gideon." Talia licked her lips. "I grabbed the knife where I assumed the killer would've gripped. The vision didn't show Alida stab either of her parents."

Gideon's powers continued to vibrate around the room, and it felt suffocating. His eyes were on the young girl at the table, not her. Alida hadn't even flinched since Gideon had barged through the door. She didn't even look up from her hands.

He'd never entered the room when she'd done her visions. Hell, she generally did her visions away from the accused. She would enter a room and touch the object in a controlled environment. When the vision ended, Talia would be aware of who the criminal was. At that point, she would see the suspect. The council had handled every aspect of the case differently, and Talia didn't like it.

"The girl did it," Gideon announced in an even tone.

Talia studied Alida for a few seconds before she glanced at Gideon. "No, she didn't. I told my vision to Arrow." She looked at the girl, and for the first time, she noticed Alida had not been secured to the table or her chair. In the past, the council would take Talia to the two-way mirror so she could identify the culprit after she'd read the object, and every suspect she'd viewed had been cuffed to the table.

Gideon released another wave of his power that almost knocked her off her feet. "I told you the girl did it," he said through gritted teeth. "Why do you insist on lying?"

How far do I want to push him? Why is he trying to wrap up the murder without a formal investigation?

Talia hated the formal investigations. She would reappear in front a judge and jury and recount every nasty thing the person had done. During the trial, she would recount her vision, and the council would show their evidence.

Talia glanced up into the corner of the room, and her heart raced. The normally red light on the camera was black. The interrogation wasn't being filmed. This was unlike the council. They did everything to protect their asses. Maybe they planned to kill Talia and blame it on the girl. Gideon looked close to killing her with his powers.

Her cases usually didn't go to formal hearings. When Gideon would confront the suspects with her vision, they would crack. Alida hadn't said a word. The only reason Talia knew what her voice sounded like was because she'd heard it in her vision.

Is the girl so dangerous that he wants to lock her up? Arrow had told Talia earlier that the girl had no powers, which Talia didn't believe. Someone had lied. Either Alida's parents had hidden her powers, or the council didn't want Talia to know about them. *But if the girl is such a threat, why didn't they handcuff her to the table?*

Talia's brow furrowed. She wished her ability to read a situation could go beyond touch. This would be an awesome time to be able to suddenly read minds.

Talia licked her lips. "That's not what I saw." Though she had never defied the council, and Gideon in particular, this time, she felt compelled to stand firm.

"What did you see?" He took a step closer. It took everything in her not to step back. Gideon's breath smelled like death, as if he was already dead inside, and when he breathed on her, she wanted to puke.

"You're telling me you weren't behind the two-way mirror when I read the girl earlier and told Arrow what I saw?" She didn't know how to explain what she saw without getting the girl in trouble.

Gideon took a menacing step forward. "I don't have to explain to you where I was. I want to know what you saw if you are so convinced she"—he pointed to Alida—"didn't do it. Who do we need to arrest?"

She wanted to beat her head against the wall. Dealing with the ancient warlock made it hurt. "Gideon, how the council found Alida doesn't make sense. How would someone know she killed her parents so fast that your men could show up when she had a knife in her hand? Furthermore, when did the council or their men ever stop me from my vision? Why did you have Arrow stop me?"

A chill came over Talia. *Does he somehow know I saw another figure in my vision? Is that why Arrow stopped me before I could figure out who or what the black figure was?* The council had never worried about her well-being in the past when her visions took a turn for the worse. *Why stop my vision this time?* The only answer she could come up with made her feel sick: the council was doing something wrong.

Gideon's normally pale face was beet red. "Are you questioning my men?"

"No, I'm not questioning your men," she said. *Not to your face, anyway.* "I'm questioning the situation. When I touched the knife, yes, I saw Alida holding it, but she didn't stab her parents." Talia stuck her chin out and held her ground.

"All I needed was to know if she held the knife in her hands."

"Then why call me if you weren't going to believe what I saw? What's different this time? You don't trust my vision? Are you going to arrest me? I held the knife also." She gestured to the knife. "You need to test the blood. I think they were dead before someone stabbed them."

She tried to remain calm, but she could feel how dangerous the situation was for the child, and her heart rushed. Her mind played out one option after another as she tried to determine the best course of action—the smartest course of action. She hadn't planned on dying that day. Talia would have preferred not to die the next day either. She hadn't even found love yet. She had never married. She had no children. Her family consisted of just her and a plant.

Gideon's eyes flash. "Are you telling me how to do my job?"

Talia shook her head. "I have no intention of telling you how to do your job. What will happen to the girl?" She jerked her head toward the child sitting in the chair, who stared sorrowfully at her hands.

"The same thing the council does with every serial killer. We might be able to rehabilitate her for one murder, but two truly blackens the soul. Can you imagine what it must be like to commit a double murder—what that must do to a soul? You can bet she's feeling the effects. She'll be dead before dawn."

Talia crossed her arms over her chest. She wanted to wrap her hands around Gideon's neck and drain the life out of him. "I'm telling you that knife"—she looked to the knife on the cart—"didn't kill her parents. I don't know how the blood got on it or how she ended up with it. But she didn't kill her parents. You need to investigate more."

As she thought about what he'd said, she wondered whether that meant his soul was black for sending so many people to their deaths. She'd never before questioned what the council did after she had her visions. But that was different—most of them had deserved to burn in the deepest part of hell.

"You are walking a fine line, Talia. Is the girl worth going to jail over?" The wind whipped around the room at Gideon's words.

"I've worked for the council for fifteen years. Have I ever questioned or not told you a vision?" When he didn't respond, she continued. "Even if she did it—which she did not—I think she deserves a fair trial."

Gideon flicked his wrist, and the silver chair she'd sat in earlier whipped against the wall with a crashing noise. "We are done here. You will not tell the council how to do their job. Furthermore, you are on thin ice, and I don't care how long you've helped us. You're paid not to ask questions."

Talia swallowed hard. She was the only one left to help this girl. Someone had murdered her parents, and Talia was the only person who felt like they needed true justice. Talia couldn't imagine dying so young. This girl had lost everything. She couldn't lose her life too—especially if she wasn't guilty.

Her mind raced. "I have another idea." Gideon's eyes glowed, but she ignored him. "Just to be sure, what if I touch her? Don't you want irrefutable evidence?"

She took a few steps closer to the girl, placing

herself between the chair and the cart. She glanced back and forth. She had never tried it before, but she wondered what would happen if she touched both at the same time.

Her fingers tingled. Talia would do whatever it took to prove the little girl innocent, even if it meant going against the council and spending a few years in jail. Talia wanted to use her gift to help the girl. The council had used it to send people to their deaths or to jail. She now had the option to help someone and prove her innocence.

Gideon took a step closer. His nostrils flared, and his black eyes glared at her as if he knew what Talia was thinking. "Don't!" he shouted, but Arrow had left the room a moment earlier, leaving just the three of them, and there was no one to pull the knife from her hand. She wasn't even sure Alida would let her touch her, but as the tips of her fingers began to wrap around the handle, the girl grabbed her hand, and there was a flash of light that completely blinded Talia. Since she didn't know what it was, and she feared for the little girl, she clutched her all the more tightly.

She was in darkness again. A wave of dizziness overcame her. Alida shushed her and pulled her into a closet. Talia's mind couldn't even process what had happened. *Where'd the closet come from?* Then she realized she wasn't in the interrogation room. She wasn't in the warehouse. *Where the hell am I?*

Beside her, Alida leaned in sadly. "My house."

"Why are we whispering?" Talia murmured, her heart full of dread.

"Because I don't know when," Alida explained calmly.

4

KIRIN

Kirin parked his Harley next to an old Toyota Corolla. His leather boots crunched on the gravel parking lot. The warehouse looked the same as always, but something was off. He didn't need to enter the building to smell fear and anger. Something had gone down, and it wasn't good. Kirin's dragon perked up at the scent of rage. He wanted to come out and play.

But just because he was immortal didn't mean he was immune to injury. The night before, a wizard had taken a chunk out of his side. Hell, being immortal didn't mean death would never come either, although it was a lot harder and required a specific method. All three of his brothers were

immortal and had dragons. Each dragon could only
die a certain way.

Gary wasn't at his normal guard post outside.
Kirin slowly entered the building, weapon drawn in
case he needed to protect himself and there wasn't
time to shift. He made it past the security desk,
which usually had a cheerful fairy behind it. He'd
had to dodge her on multiple occasions as she tried
to throw glitter on him. Kirin's dragon wanted to eat
her for her cheerfulness and need to spread glitter.
He passed into the inner sanctum, where the TVs on
the back wall played the local news, and then toward
the white hallway, his Glock in his hand. Gideon,
Arrow, and Kael—the second in command—were
all storming down the hall toward him. He glanced
behind him, but no, they were definitely trying to
meet up with Kirin.

"What's going on?" Kirin asked quietly.

"One of our trusted psychics escaped with a fugitive. I will pay you double the usual price. You have
two targets to bring in. Follow me." Gideon wasn't
even trying to control his powers.

Kirin leaned over to Kael as they followed
Gideon down the hall. "Why is no one in the
building?"

Kael looked at Gideon's back. "Gideon lost his

temper when the fugitive escaped. I thought it would be better to send everyone home."

Kirin followed Gideon down the hall to his office. The white walls closed in around him, and his brother's voice rang through his mind about doing the job for the money. Maybe it was time to ask questions.

Gideon swung open the door to his office with a flick of his hand. No matter how many times he set foot in Gideon's office, Kirin felt transported back in time to the Renaissance era. Gideon had been around for a thousand years. The Renaissance must have been his favorite time, because he'd painted the walls in dark, rich blues and reds, depicting a village of women and children looking off into the distance as a warlock burned the surrounding area to ashes. Kirin wondered if the warlock was Gideon.

Gideon sat in the high-back leather chair and nodded for Kirin to take one of the two chairs in front of the large dark wooden desk. He continued to keep his hands inside his robe. The only contemporary thing in the room was the Apple computer on his desk. Kirin wondered if Gideon took his hands out of the robe to use it.

"Can you tell me who I'm after?" Kirin's dragon paced around, wanting out. In the past three hundred years, his dragon had never been this agitated.

Arrow walked over to the computer and turned the monitor so that Kirin could see. An image of a beautiful woman flashed across the screen. Her blue eyes shone as she looked at the camera. Whoever had taken the picture must have made her laugh. Her smile looked real, not faked for a photo. She had to be in her midthirties. Her long blond hair was tied up, and she wore a black T-shirt that was tight and accented her breasts. Kirin wondered what it would be like to feel them in his hands. His dragon immediately yelled *Mine!* in his mind. Kirin couldn't help but roll his eyes. She was not theirs. They were going to bring her in for justice.

Arrow's voice brought him out of his trance. "Talia has worked for the council for fifteen years."

"What's her gift?"

"She can touch an object and get a vision. The visions can be past, present, or future, whatever is strongest."

Kirin glanced back at the photo. "What did she do?"

Gideon rose from his chair and paced behind the desk. "It doesn't matter what she did. I want her back in my custody by morning."

"I would like to understand what I'm heading into."

The air became thick in the room. Gideon's eyes turned pitch-black. "All you need to know is she can get visions, and I want her back here."

Once again, Kirin's brother's words floated through his mind. *Ask more questions. Did this Talia ask too many questions? What did she do to mess up so badly, and how can someone with visions overpower the three men in the room and escape?*

The screen flicked to a new picture of an adorable girl who couldn't have been more than eight years old. Her curly blond locks were in pigtails. Kirin hoped Gideon didn't expect him to bring in a young girl. He would need more information.

"She's a little girl," he noted.

Gideon put his hands on the desk and leaned over. This was the first time Kirin had seen him take his hands out of his robes.

"She's a murderer. Killed her parents." Kael stared at her picture, a flicker of emotion passing over his face so quickly that Kirin would have missed it if he hadn't been watching closely.

"Is this going to be a problem?" Gideon asked.

Kirin shook his head. "No, sir." He continued, "Does the girl have powers?"

"No," Gideon replied too fast.

Kirin rolled his head. "How did they escape?"

Kael stepped forward, and Gideon raised his hands. "It doesn't matter how they escaped. I want them back."

Kael shook his head. It seemed he didn't like the way Gideon was handling things. If Kirin ran into trouble, he would call Kael.

Arrow handed him a folder with the information they'd printed out for him. Kirin knew he wouldn't get any more out of Gideon. He stood and walked back down the plain hallway. It seemed strange with no one in the warehouse. As he exited the room, his mind was still wrapped around the question of how a young girl and a psychic had escaped. He didn't want to take the case, but he knew if he passed on it, one of the other mercenaries would pick it up and not ask questions. His brother's words still wormed around in his mind. Yesterday, he would have hunted down the woman and the girl and not thought twice about it. Now he had this bad feeling in the pit of his stomach.

He stuffed the paperwork into the bike's saddle-bag. Then he hopped on, pulled on his gloves, and drove to his thinking spot on the top of the cliff over-looking the city. Sometimes he'd go there to relax, and other times, he'd strip down and spread his wings. From up there, Haven Springs looked beautiful, serene, and safe.

He parked the bike, pulled out the paperwork, and started to read through it. It wasn't easy to read the information on the girl—someone had blacked out a majority of the things he needed to know. The little girl had no noted abilities, yet she'd somehow managed to escape council custody. The woman had only psychic abilities, and... they'd left together. Something wasn't right. Someone was lying.

Kirin shook his head. He'd worked for Gideon for more than a hundred years. If Gideon had done something wrong, Kirin would have figured it out by now. And since the females had run, his money was on them being the ones who had done something illegal. And since Gideon was paying double, Kirin's motivation was at an all-time high. Factoring in the birthday party he had to attend the next day, this had to be a rush job. He would collect the woman and the girl and let Gideon worry about the punish-ment. Kirin wouldn't miss his brother's birthday because of this.

He tried to figure out where to look. He had the

address of the woman's apartment and the little girl's home. Though both were long shots, that was what he had to go on. Maybe he'd pick up a scent, and it would help him in his quest. As he started the bike, he groaned. He'd forgotten to pick up his pay from the last job. That was a mistake, but he'd remedy it the next day when he cashed in on this one.

The woman's apartment was on the way to the girl's. Kirin pointed his bike in that direction. Twenty minutes later, he was parked in front of an apartment in the middle of Haven Springs. Kirin didn't come into town often. The town was fifty percent supernatural, and the humans didn't know who lived among them, but almost everyone knew everyone.

Kirin didn't bother knocking on the door. He used the card in his pocket to push the lock back. When he entered the woman's house, her vanilla scent assaulted him. His dragon perked at the smell and wanted to find the woman it belonged to. Kirin wanted the same thing for a separate reason—he planned for a nice payout.

The color pink was everywhere. The couch, blankets, and even the walls were in shades of pink. Kirin walked through the living room and a small kitchen that looked like she never used it. The door down the hall was closed. He twisted the handle and opened it to find another room that looked like pink had thrown up in it. He didn't know how someone could buy so much of one color.

But when he scanned the room, he couldn't tear his eyes away from the framed photo on the dresser. It showed a small cabin in the background, with the woman he was looking for and an older woman standing in front. The younger woman's head was thrown back as she laughed.

Kirin walked into the closet, looking for a sign that she had come here after running. All he saw were mounds of high heels. Kirin didn't understand someone who would spend all her money on shoes. Now, *gold*—that was a good investment. His dragon agreed with him.

Kirin walked back through the apartment, disappointed that his first stop hadn't given him more information. When he left the apartment, an older lady was standing in the hallway, her gray hair pulled into a bun. A pair of sunglasses covered her eyes.

"What are you doing in Talia's apartment?" she asked.

"I was checking on the place for her."

The older lady cocked her head. "What are you?"

Kirin quickly put his sunglasses on. He had taken them off when he entered the apartment. This case had his dragon close to the surface, making his eyes glow bright gold. "I'm just a friend of Talia's."

She shook her finger in his direction. "I know you aren't her friend. And when she leaves, I look after her house. Now, what are you, and what have you done to my Talia?"

He walked over to the elderly lady. "I work for someone who's looking for her. If Talia comes back, call me."

"Ha. I will tell her to run. I've told her to stop working for the council for years. I tell you, that Gideon is bad news."

It wasn't normal to speak about the supernatural world in public. Kirin scanned the surrounding area before answering. "Please call."

The old lady removed her sunglasses, and her eyes glowed purple. "Gold won't keep you warm at night." Before Kirin could ask her another question, she disappeared—one second she was standing in front of him, and the next, she was nowhere to be seen. Kirin didn't have time to figure out what she was. He needed to find Talia.

When Kirin walked outside, a figure in a dark robe was standing next to his bike. Kirin couldn't hold back the groan. The man wore the same robe as the warlock he'd fought the previous day.

Kirin walked toward the warlock, pulling his power from his dragon. "You want to explain why you're touching my bike?"

When the warlock looked at him, Kirin was stunned for a second. The man looked identical to the one he'd just gone after. But that couldn't be true. Kia had told him that the council sentenced that warlock to death the night before.

The warlock pulled his hand from the bike. "I'm looking for my brother."

"Sorry, that's not his bike—it's mine."

The warlock stepped in his direction. "I know it's not my brother's bike. But it was the last image he portrayed. Now, tell me where my brother is."

Kirin let out a sigh. "You need to contact Gideon about your brother."

Kirin glanced around the parking lot, making sure no humans were near. The warlock looked close to using his magic. Kirin really didn't want to fill out any paperwork for a fight with a warlock in an open parking lot.

"You are a mercenary." It wasn't a question as much as a statement.

"My job was to bring him in."

The warlock crossed his arms. "Did Gideon give you a reason?"

"No."

The man rolled his eyes. "Leave it to a mercenary to not ask questions and bring his charge in."

Why does everyone suddenly want me to analyze every case I take?

"So everyone keeps saying. If I hear anything, I will let you know."

"On your way to bring another innocent person in?"

Before Kirin had time to reply, the warlock vanished. Kirin let out a sigh, got back on his motorcycle, and sent his brother a text about the visitor he'd encountered. It was time to find the young girl's house, which was ten miles outside of town. The cool air felt good as he sped down the highway toward his next target. Kirin cut the engine early when he noticed a light on inside the house.

Maybe his payday would come quickly, and he could make it to his brother's birthday. But the idea of doing this mission for money left a bad taste in his mouth.

5

TALIA

They sat silently for over an hour. In fact, it was probably longer, since they'd both dozed off. Talia leaned forward, cracked the closet door, and peeked out. She could see the knife on the floor. Talia shivered at the sight of the caked-on blood. When they arrived at Alida's house, Talia had immediately dropped the knife. An overwhelming urge to sleep had overtaken her before Alida pulled her into the closet. The vision from earlier, along with whatever Alida had done, drained what energy she had. She couldn't chance touching the knife again.

Alida tugged at her shirt. When Talia sat back down, Alida snuggled in close to her. Talia was certain that if she started to touch things in the closet, the drained feeling would only get worse. At a young age, she'd learned to wear gloves, except for when she worked for the council. In the middle of summer, people stared, but she'd learned to ignore the looks. When she went to school, kids made fun of her. One day, she couldn't stand the teasing, and she didn't wear her gloves. That morning, when she handed her teacher an assignment, her hand brushed his, and the vision that appeared still haunted her. He had broken his wife's arm that morning for not having the coffee started. The cops didn't believe her when she ran to the station to report him. Until the council called, she'd never tried to help anyone again. Humans didn't understand when she couldn't explain how she knew something.

She reached into her back pocket, pulled out a pair of cloth gloves, and slipped them over her hands. Talia had used all her energy earlier and couldn't chance another vision. She needed to stay alert. There was no doubt in her mind that it was only a matter of time before the council sent one of their men after them. Over the years, she'd seen the mercenaries the council called. They radiated danger, and the only thing they cared about was the money for each person they brought in. Talia had never heard of them caring about anything else.

"What do you think will happen next?" Alida whispered.

Talia took a deep breath. She wanted to lie and tell the girl everything would be okay, but Talia felt deep down that things would get worse. "Well, my guess is they will have someone look for us."

"Like who?" Alida squeezed her arms around Talia.

"They generally hire mercenaries. Do you know what a mercenary is?"

Alida shook her head.

"Someone who only cares about money and will do any job for it." Talia shrugged like it was no big deal, but she was afraid. Those out for money wouldn't care about the truth. Mercenaries would never believe she'd simply touched the girl and then disappeared, and even if they did believe it, they wouldn't care. Mercenaries only wanted one thing: payday. Talia feared the council would send Kirin after them. Everyone in the supernatural world knew him as someone who captured anyone the council sent him after. She had seen him in passing. If he weren't so hot, she would hate his guts. He drove a slick black motorcycle, and his hair was always tousled from the breeze. His gold eyes captured her every time. She knew he had no clue who she was, but when Talia saw him, she wanted to wrap her legs around his waist.

Talia banished the daydream to concentrate on the little girl in front of her. "Do you know how we got here?"

"Yes. I can transport, but sometimes I move backward or forward in time."

"Did your mom and dad know?"

The little girl tightened her hold on Talia's waist. "Yes. Mommy always told me to keep it a secret. Mommy normally gave me a pill every morning that helped me not transport. But I didn't get my pill, so now my magic works."

Talia understood why her mother didn't want anyone to know about her daughter's ability. The council would use the girl's ability for their gain. Transporting in time could be dangerous. She needed to make sure to grab the medicine and figure out where Alida's parents had it made. Nobody could ever find out about the girl's ability.

"Alida, tell nobody you can move back and forth in time. They will think you can transport, but they don't need to know you can move through time."

"Okay," she murmured.

"Stay here. I'm going to check this out." Talia was still worried they might be at the wrong point in time.

Even though the little girl nodded, her eyes started to fill with tears. Talia wanted to pull the girl into her arms and promise her everything would be okay. But instead of giving the girl a hug and wiping the tears away, Talia exited the closet and pulled out her phone. She had a missed call from her neighbor, Ms. Bethlow, who needed her to pick something up from the store. The date flashed, and she let out a breath. They hadn't moved through time.

Talia wandered around Alida's room, trying to understand who would come after the family. The girl's room was the key to her heart. The twin-bed frame was pink, and there was a pink netting over the bed. The wall behind the bed was a painted picture of the princess from Mario Brothers. Talia left the girl's room and entered the first door to the right, moving into another bedroom, this one clean and neat with a light-blue bedspread. It looked like a guest room. The next room was a bathroom, so Talia continued down the hall to the last bedroom.

When she opened the door to the master bedroom, her heart hurt. The left wall was covered in family pictures. The three looked so happy, and in the ones that showed Alida looking at her parents, her face was lit up. Even though Talia couldn't get a good vision of the parents' death, she knew Alida couldn't have done it. The master bedroom was tidy. On the dresser sat a jewelry box full of gold necklaces and expensive rings. There was no sign that someone had burglarized the place. She sighed. Of course, that would have been too easy. Talia closed the door and headed downstairs.

The main floor was a different story. Blood covered the walls, so much of it everywhere. The copper scent made Talia choke, and she had to cover her mouth so she could breathe. On a closer look, she saw blood spattering the ceiling. There was no way a little girl could do this much to an adult. Talia reached into her pocket and pulled out her phone to take pictures. If she couldn't get a good vision, she would need to get evidence to prove the girl innocent.

She wasn't even touching objects, and the emotions were washing over her. Fear. Anguish. Rage. The attack had taken place in the kitchen at the back of the house. An infomercial for a purse played on the living room television. Talia followed the trail of blood to the back kitchen, where she saw two voids in the blood on the floor. The council had removed the bodies when they came for the girl. Hadn't anyone looked at the scene? She was rather glad Alida hadn't transported them to the middle of her parents being murdered. If that had happened, she and the girl might both be dead by now.

Talia didn't want to touch the blood in the kitchen yet. She wanted to see the rest of the downstairs. Talia moved around the main floor until she reached the office at the front of the house. The desktop computer was in sleep mode. She hoped Alida's parents hadn't password protected it. Talia wiggled the mouse to bring the computer to life. Sadly, her hope for an unlocked computer was struck down. She figured she might make one or two guesses and not risk the hard drive deleting. She glanced around for some clue. All around were pictures of the family and Alida. *It can't be that easy, can it?* She typed in "Alida." Wrong. Then she glanced at a framed birth certificate. Alida and her birthdate. *Ding-ding-ding!*

The desk was a mess, drawers partially open, the papers on top not in order. She needed to ask Alida later if that was normal.

"It's not," Alida murmured from the door.

Talia couldn't help screaming. "What are you doing down here?"

Alida sighed. "I didn't want to be alone. What if he came back?"

This was new. "Who?"

She looked at the ground. "I'm not sure. When he showed up, my parents sent me to my room before they even opened the door. I never saw him. I just heard voices. And screams."

"I know this is hard, but I need you to think really hard. Did you hear them say anything?"

Alida hugged herself. "Dad talked to someone when they walked toward the kitchen. My dad knew the person, I heard him greet the man, but I couldn't catch his name. Once they were in the kitchen, I heard screams."

Talia licked her lips. "Did you hear him go anywhere else?"

"Yes, he came in here. Then he left. I didn't come down until I heard his motorcycle start."

Alida had just given them another piece of the puzzle. They now knew the guy drove a motorcycle. Talia slowly took off her gloves. She needed to get more rest, but time would run out soon. The mercenary would be on his way to Alida's house, looking for them.

Talia ran her hands over the keyboard. No vision came. *That can't be right.* She touched the keyboard again. Nothing. She reached for the pen on the desk. Nothing. Then she looked at Alida.

"Daddy had a witch protect his office. You won't get a vision."

She sat down in the chair and looked around. *What could be so important he would spell his office?* If she couldn't get a read on anything on the house, she would see if Alida could send them into the past. She needed answers to clear the little girl and herself.

"I'm not good at gauging time. I could have sent us to the future or the past. I could never pinpoint a time."

"Alida, do you also read minds? Nothing I've said was out loud."

"It just happened today. I don't know how to stop." Alida's eyes watered.

"I'm not mad at you for reading my mind. Earlier, when we were in the interrogation room, did you read Gideon's mind?"

"No. It didn't happen until we came here."

Talia slipped her gloves back on and made her way out of the office. Alida grabbed her hand and walked with her to the kitchen. The smell of copper was the strongest in this room, but there was another smell too. Talia wished she had shifter smell ability so she could pick up what it was.

She glanced around the room and didn't know where to start. She dropped Alida's hand, removed her gloves again, and took a deep breath before touching the white countertop. Maya, Alida's mother, was at the stove stirring a pot of red sauce. The spoon and sauce still sat on the stove top. Maya had the most beautiful smile, and she laughed at something Alida said. Alida's mother was in midsentence when the doorbell rang, just as Alida had said.

The counter didn't give Talia the answers she needed to find out who'd killed Alida's parents. She dreaded it, but the only thing left to touch was Maya's blood. She reached out and was bracing for the pain when Alida rushed to her side.

"Someone's here!" she squealed.

Talia looked up and saw the mercenary. He frowned as he peeled off his sunglasses. For a moment, she lost herself in his eyes, which glowed bright gold. Before Talia had time to process the mercenary in the kitchen, Alida threw her arms around her neck, and they transported in a flash of light again.

6

KIRIN

Kirin parked his motorcycle in the driveway and stretched his legs. His neck and back ached with tension. When he glanced up, he saw the white picket fence of Alida's house.

Kirin unlatched the gate and walked up to the front door. He twisted the handle, but someone had locked the house. Kirin reached into his back pocket to pull out his lock-pick set. It only took a couple of seconds, and he had the door open. He'd learned his lock-picking skill decades before.

His dragon picked up the sound of someone in the kitchen. This job wouldn't be too hard. Death had a scent. It was different for every person. Kirin had seen so many people die over the years that he was aware of the scent instantly. It affected each person differently. For most people, it would trigger a sad moment from the past—a grandfather or grandmother passing or even a beloved pet. For Kirin, it triggered the moment his father had died battling the Damasus Dragons. They were pure evil and wanted to rule the world. When they killed his father, Kirin vowed to eliminate every Damasus dragon. He spent the next three decades eliminating any dragon who'd had a part in his father's death. Even though the power-hungry dragons had killed his father two hundred years before, the memory still haunted him.

Kirin banished the memory of his father's death. He took a couple of seconds to glance around the living room. A picture of the family on the wall caught his eye. He recognized the little girl's father, Jalil Meadows, who'd been in charge of the labs in the dungeon, which Kirin had always tried to stay away from.

He continued through the living room toward the kitchen. Kirin removed his sunglasses to take a look at the woman and the girl, but his charges vanished in a literal flash before he had time to set the sunglasses back on his head. His eyes burned from the light, blinded for a second.

"Fuck," Kirin mumbled to the empty room as he recovered from the blinding light. *There goes wrapping the case up quickly and getting home to my hoard and watching Monday night football.*

With his sunglasses back on, Kirin stared at the spot where the two had been. He couldn't believe a little girl and some woman had bested him. And he couldn't shake the feeling that he knew the woman.

Kirin walked over to where they'd both stood and shook his head. The moment the little girl's eyes had landed on him, she'd wrapped her arms around the beautiful woman, and they'd disappeared. Gideon had said nothing about them being able to vanish. *Doesn't he think that information would be relevant for bringing them in?*

Kirin pulled out the paper on the psychic from his back pocket. He glanced down the sheet. Nothing —not one word about transportation powers. He didn't even bother with the young girl's paper, since the council had blacked out most of it, stating that her father's information was classified. Now he understood how they'd escaped the council. Kirin couldn't hold back a smile, imagining Gideon's reaction when the two disappeared in front of him. The young girl and sexy woman had an advantage over the council.

Where did that come from? His dragon had perked up at the mention of the sexy woman. But no matter how beautiful she was, he would bring her in and go to his brother's birthday party.

In the past hundred years, Kirin had never had to bring in a person who could transport. He had met no one with that ability. He let out a chuckle. He'd been beaten by a little girl.

The woman and child flashed through his mind. They'd both been both pale and shaken. The girl didn't look like she was capable of killing. And the woman looked afraid, not like someone who had deliberately gone against the orders of the council. And something else—he remembered the haunted look in the woman's eyes... *Talia*.

Talia, his dragon mumbled in his mind.

When he'd entered the room, the woman was touching the blood. She'd told the council the girl was innocent. *Why did she come back to the crime scene and touch the blood?* Kirin wondered what the psychic had seen when she felt the blood. Kirin felt certain, deep down, that she wasn't trying to cover anything up. The woman had looked determined to receive a vision from the blood.

With a frown, he decided to check out the rest of the house. When he looked up, he noticed blood spatter on the ceiling. The more he scrutinized the case, the less sense it made. Kirin had killed people over the years. Using a knife, there was no way the little girl had the strength to cause the blood spatter on the ceiling. He let out a frustrated breath. He usually didn't pay attention to the crime scene unless it gave him an insight into where his escapee might be. But his brother's words echoed in his mind.

Kirin took the stairs two at a time and swung the first door open. The room must have belonged to the little girl. He walked around, taking in her toys. Nothing screamed the location they might have transported to. The two of them might be anywhere.

Nothing upstairs gave him information about what could help him find the girl and woman. He headed back downstairs. He would try to obtain an idea of potential locations by first sniffing around here. And yes, he partially meant *inhaling*. His sense of smell was highly sensitive. At the moment, blood overwhelmed his senses with the metallic scent. Talia had been touching it. Maybe that would help him find them.

He checked out the main floor then the rest of

the house. The girl and the woman had been all over and left the house mostly undisturbed. Kirin knew this because the scent clinging to the mess belonged to someone else. What bothered him was that he recognized the smell and knew he'd met with the person to whom it belonged, but he couldn't remember who that was.

Giving up, Kirin decided to go check out the psychic's place again. *Talia*, his dragon purred. He liked the way her name sounded on his tongue. Immediately, he regretted that thought. He needed to stop thinking of her as anything other than a job. She was a paycheck. And if he didn't capture her soon, she'd be keeping him from his brother's birthday. As ridiculous as he thought it was to celebrate, he relished the opportunity to see his brothers and mom again. They needed to stick together because they were all the family any of them had left.

As three bachelor brothers, at their ages, they might just be the last of their line. That thought ate at him when he slowed down long enough to think about it—which was a good enough reason now for him to pick up the pace and get moving. He took one last look around the house, confident they weren't hidden there, and made his way back out to his bike.

He opened his saddlebag and checked out the file then left for Talia's house.

The ride was long. The day was growing late, and as the sun set, he pulled off his dark glasses to see better. He normally left them on because, at night, his eyes would pick up the light from oncoming vehicles and reflect back at them like a wild animal. He had caused more than one accident that way. But out in the hills of West Virginia, far from civilization, he felt safe enough to remove them and relax into the ride. Kirin loved the way the wind whipped over his skin. It made him feel alive. Though he'd lived more than three hundred years, he hadn't felt truly alive for far too long.

Kirin considered how to approach the woman and girl. He'd captured a lot of different kinds of supernatural creatures in the time he'd worked as a mercenary. From a young age, his dad had prepared him for violence, so being attacked never worried Kirin. It was just another occupational hazard. But he was in uncertain territory, because he'd never had people disappear on him. He wondered how to keep it from happening again. If he couldn't, this chase would go on forever.

Kirin pulled his motorcycle over and pulled out

his phone. Maybe Kia would know something about a supernatural who could disappear.

Kia answered on the first ring. "Kirin."

"I need your help. Have you ever come across someone on the Internet with the ability that one minute they were present, and the next, there was a flash of light, and they disappeared?" Kirin ran a hand through his hair.

Kia laughed on the other end. "I'm a tech genius. I'm not Google. Try looking it up online."

Kirin shuddered. "I don't know how. The idea of Google makes me want to break out in hives."

"And this is why so many dragons shifters have died out. You have to keep up with technology."

"Just look it up, and tell me what I need to know. I'll wait," Kirin said angrily.

Kirin could hear Kia's fingers typing on the keyboard. Kia would have an answer for him. Kirin didn't correct his brother on why the dragon shifters had died out. That was an argument he wasn't in the mood to have. The dragon shifters had died out because so many of them wanted to rule the world and thought they were more important than humans. Shifters needed to live a balance between the supernatural world and the human world.

"I just checked my normal site on the dark web.

There is only one person documented who could transport, and he died years ago."

Kirin didn't believe there was only one other person who could transport. That was a supernatural power the council would love. He figured that anyone else who could transport hid it from the world. He didn't blame them—it just made his job harder.

"Fuck," Kirin mumbled. "The little girl I'm after teleports when I get close. I need to figure out a way to find them."

Kia let out a sigh. "You're going after a little girl. What could she have possible done that the council wants her for? I bet they figured out her powers and want to use her. Do you understand what you might do to this girl?"

"Yes!" Kirin yelled. "But I need to find them before the council sends someone else. Just because I don't look for them doesn't mean Gideon won't send another team after her."

"Good to know you still have a moral compass. I will keep looking for a way to find them. But you'd better hurry, because it will upset Conley if you miss his birthday, and Mom comes in tomorrow."

Kirin hung up, knowing that Kia would rat him out to their mother. He couldn't help feeling that something was off. He needed to find the woman and child before Gideon sent someone else. The thought of Gideon using his council power to bring the girl in didn't sit well with Kirin or his dragon. When he glanced at the mirror on his bike, his eyes were glowing bright gold. He would need to wear his sunglasses for the rest of the drive.

7

TALIA

Talia opened her eyes, and her heart pounded. This was bad really bad. Alida had sent them to the one place they needed to avoid.

"I'm sorry," Alida whispered. "Your mind went blank."

Fuck. Talia looked down at the little girl. Alida fortunately hadn't listened to her internal monologue. "This is bad."

The sound of the doorknob turning cut her off. Kael walked in, talking on the phone. When his eyes landed on her and Alida, he held up a finger. "Gideon, I will meet you in your office in ten. I need to make a call."

Talia let out her breath. She didn't always like

Kael, but she didn't think he was a bad guy. He would know something.

"What are you doing here?" Kael ground out.

"I'm sorry, Kael. I messed up."

He took two giant steps across the room and wrapped his arms around Alida. "You guys need to get out of here. Talia, I figured you would try to prove her innocence, not bring her back here." Talia didn't know how he could growl at her and be so gentle with the young girl. She couldn't hold back her anger. "You know about her powers. Why aren't you helping her?"

"I've worked hard with her parents to keep her powers a secret. There is more going on than meets the eye. You know how hard it was for me to get Gideon to let you come to the council in the beginning? He believes his henchmen when they say that Alida killed her parents. He was close to her dad—well, he thought he was, anyway. Jalil hated what Gideon did and normally went behind his back. Gideon is mad because he didn't know about the girl's powers."

"A heads-up would've been nice."

The warlock shrugged. Talia knew he didn't care what happened to her. He was only trying to help the girl.

"I need you to take Alida and protect her with your life," he said. "You need to go on the run."

Talia collapsed into Kael's chair. "Gideon called Kirin. The council's top tracker is on my trail."

"You're welcome."

"How is Kirin coming after me helpful?"

Kael paced his office with Alida in his arms and rubbed her back. The girl had dozed off on his shoulder. "He is the best mercenary we have, but he also has a conscience. If he sees something off, he will work to find the cause.

"We need to prove her innocence, Talia. I need your help." Kael put Alida on her lap before he walked over to his door and locked it. "We don't have much time. Gideon will be looking for me soon. I'm working on something, but I need you to keep her safe." Kael knelt in front of her chair. He shook Alida until her eyes opened. "Hey, my little telly. I need you to take Talia somewhere. Be safe. I will contact you when I know the council is no longer looking for you."

Alida reached forward and hugged Kael. "Okay."

Alida wrapped her arms around Talia's neck and closed her eyes. Nothing happened.

"Come on, Alida. We have little time," Kael said.

She closed her eyes again. Nothing. "It's not

working." Her bottom lip started to shake the same time that someone pounded on the door.

"Kael, open your door."

"One second, Gideon." Kael turned his attention back to the young girl. "I know you can do this." Someone slipped the key into the door. Alida tightened her hold and closed her eyes one more time. Talia saw the doorknob to Kael's office turn just as they disappeared.

When Talia's head finally stopped pounding and she opened her eyes, she realized that she was in her apartment with Alida. She glanced around. Something was off. It felt like someone had been there. Talia looked at the door. The lock was engaged.

She let out a breath. "Why here?"

Alida's head hung. "It was the only place I saw in your mind that I could get to. I tried others." All Talia had been thinking since she ended up at the office was that she wanted to go home. Granted, there wasn't much for her to come home to, but at least she had a place to go. And Alida had picked this out of her mind. Talia blamed it on the girl's tiredness.

"What else can you do?" Talia asked as she studied the little girl.

Alida shook her head. "We're not supposed to talk about it."

Talia wrapped Alida in her arms and sat down on the couch. "Alida, I understand your parents said not to talk about your powers, but I need to know what you can do. I will tell no one. I pinky swear." Talia held out her pinky, waiting to see what Alida would do. The little girl smiled and hooked her pinky around Talia's. "It is important that you tell no one you don't trust."

Alida fiddled with the pink tassels on the couch pillow. "I trust you."

Her declaration warmed Talia's heart. Talia didn't know what the next few hours held for them, but she would do everything in her power to make sure Alida was taken care of.

"Okay, I need to know what else you can do."

"One time, my mommy was crying. I could see an image in her head of her holding an older woman's hand. When I touched my mommy, I transported us to the image. I didn't know it was ten years ago."

"Have you traveled to a different time when you didn't see a picture?"

Talia and Alida already had enough on their plate. She didn't need to be traveling to different points in time. *Who knows how long it would take to get us back to the correct time?*

"I was mad at Mom once and tried to transport to my room. I thought of an object in my room, but Mom threw it away a few years earlier. It took me a day to get to the right time. When I did, Mom and Dad were panicking. That was when they called on a witch to create my medicine."

So someone outside of her family knew about her powers. "Alida, could this witch kill your parents?"

"No. Rysa would never hurt my mom and dad. Do you want to go to her house? She lives in Cassadaga, Florida."

Talia discarded that idea. She didn't know this person and didn't want to put anyone else in harm's way.

"Let's stay here and come up with a plan. Do you feel okay being off your medication?"

"It's been a year since I started to take the pills. I can feel the strength of my powers. I can't just see images in your mind—I can hear what you're thinking."

"Okay. If possible, don't read my mind unless we are in danger." Talia didn't need the little girl learning every curse word in existence.

Alida let out a giggle. "My daddy would slip curse words every so often."

Talia worried about not having Alida's medication. No doubt, as members of the council, they knew the dangers of raising a child who was too different—a kid who didn't fit into any box.

Talia had removed her gloves when they sat down on the couch. She still had one glove off when she hugged Alida close without thinking, and the minute she touched the little girl's skin, images assaulted her. A perfect family played out like a movie. Jalil and Maya, Alida's parents, hugged her at the end of the street. In the distance, she could see a yellow school bus.

Maya pulled back and held Alida's hands. "Now, remember what we talked about."

Alida rolled her brown eyes. "I know, Mom. I'm special, and other people don't have powers."

Maya glanced up at her husband. "It's not only the council we worry about. Humans don't know about us."

"Mom, this isn't the first year of me going to school. I'm eight years old. I know you and Daddy are the only ones I can talk to about my powers. Plus, the magic pills make it so I can't use my powers."

Jalil looked down at his daughter with so much

pride. "Alida, we know you are strong. Your mom and I worry that if you get in a bad situation, you might still be able to use your powers. Please be careful. You are our everything. Your mom and I will do everything in our power to protect you."

"I know, Daddy, but the bus is coming, and I don't want the other kids to make fun of me for you guys standing here."

Maya let out a chuckle. "Of course, dear. Remember, if anything is off, please use the phone and call us. Trust no one but your mom and dad. I know you've met people at the council, but don't trust them. Your powers are far greater than anyone can imagine, and who knows what the council will do."

"Okay." The last image was Alida hugging her parents.

Talia pulled her hand away from the girl. She leaned back on her couch and closed her eyes for a second. She could feel the love pouring off of Alida's parents in the vision. Talia could also feel the love Alida had for her parents. She understood the parents' worry. Her gut tightened at the thought of Gideon finding out about the girl's powers.

Talia had grown up with normal parents who had no powers. Her mom was a descendant of psychics but hadn't inherited the power. But she'd passed it down. Talia's parents lectured her for hours about keeping her powers a secret. The council worried her mom, who thought they would take Talia away because neither of her parents had powers.

When Talia was eighteen, someone killed her parents in a car accident. A couple of months later, Gideon showed up at her door. He informed her that her parents had arranged for a letter to be delivered to him upon their death and that he was there to help her. But Gideon never helped her over the years. He used her power to help bring down punishment. Talia wondered if what he'd said was true but stopped quickly because her head hurt too much to go down the path of thinking about her parents.

Talia put her gloves back on and pulled Alida to her feet. The girl yawned, and her eyes kept shutting. She was completely worn out and could hardly move. Talia grabbed her under the armpits and picked her up. She took a few quick steps down the hall and tucked her into bed.

Her stomach growled as she headed toward the kitchen. Talia didn't know if she would keep her eyes open as she made dinner. With a quick survey of her cabinets, she noticed a jar of peanut butter. In the fridge, she found a jar of grape jelly, so she made peanut butter and jelly sandwiches. On the counter sat a bag of sour cream and onion chips. When she put the jelly back in the fridge, she noticed a carton of milk. After a quick check of the date, she let out a sigh.

Sandwich chips and milk in hand, Talia headed back toward the bedroom. She glanced at her phone to check the time. It was well after midnight. Guilt washed over her as she saw that she had a missed call and voice mail. Her neighbor had no one to rely on but her. She hoped Ms. Bethlow was okay. It would be terrible if something happened to her. But it was too late to call her. She made a mental reminder to check on Ms. Bethlow first thing in the morning.

Pushing the door open with her foot, she couldn't help but smile at the little girl wrapped up in her pink comforter. Alida was sound asleep, her little arms wrapped around Talia's stuffed panda-corn. Talia placed the sandwich and chips on the nightstand. She walked over and closed the blinds. On her way out, she turned the light off and took one more look at the young girl. Talia would do anything to protect her from the evil in the world, and that included going against the council.

Cleaning up the kitchen took a matter of seconds. She ran a cloth over the counter and let the day sink in. Talia had gotten a good look at the mercenary before Alida transported them out of her house. She had a feeling Gideon knew more than he let on. There was no reason Gideon would send Kirin after them unless he was worried about what Alida could do. She thought about sexy-as-hell Kirin in his leather boots, wearing a polo shirt that molded to his muscles, his hair messy from riding his motorcycle...

What am I doing, daydreaming about a man who is only after us for a paycheck? If Gideon had sent Kirin after them, he'd probably had his tech guy freeze her bank account and credit card. She wouldn't be surprised if they'd marked her car as stolen and had her driver's license revoked. Talia had always worried she might need to run one day, but she'd never planned for it. She never carried cash. Now she worried she wouldn't be able to get food for Alida. She planned to let the girl sleep a little longer before they transported anywhere else. She needed to come up with a place the mercenary wouldn't think to look.

Perhaps most importantly, she had to figure out how to prove that Alida was innocent. If she could do that, she had a chance of fixing her life and Alida's. If she couldn't, then they were both as good as dead. She couldn't let that happen to the sweet little girl.

Talia decided to have Alida transport them to her cabin. Once she had Alida tucked away there, she would take a car and work on solving her case.

It had been over an hour when Talia crept back into the room. Alida was still sound asleep. Talia grabbed a blanket off the bed and sat down on the floor. She didn't realize she'd fallen asleep until something startled her awake. Her eyes opened wide, and she realized she was staring into the face of Kirin.

She opened her mouth to scream, to warn Alida and give her a chance to get away, but Kirin shook his head and motioned for her to come with him. Then he held out a hand to help her off the floor. She took it and braced herself as memories washed over her.

8

KIRIN

Kirin found them. The moment he opened Talia's door, his dragon scented her and the girl in the house. It shocked him that the two fugitives would hide in Talia's home. *Who comes back to their house when they're on the run?* They had to be the worst criminals in history.

His gut tightened. If he didn't bring them in soon, Gideon would send out another set of mercenaries. The thought of someone else taking Talia into custody bothered him. But Kirin had no time to deal with his feelings.

The soft snore of the little girl echoed through the house. Kirin followed the sound down the hall toward Talia's bedroom. He shook his head as he opened up the door and saw both fugitives lying there fast asleep. If the doubt hadn't already started setting in, the sight of the two of them asleep in Talia's bedroom would have been a clue that they were both innocent. But they still needed to find evidence to prove their innocence. That was why the council set up laws. Running wasn't an option. They needed to go on trial like everyone else.

As he squatted before her, Talia opened her hazel eyes. They held so much fear. He could tell her brain had gone into overdrive trying to figure out a way to escape. As long as he kept her from the little girl, she couldn't get away. But with one look in her fear-filled eyes, he wanted to take her and the girl to his house and protect them both. That wasn't a regular thought on his part. He normally liked no one other than himself inside his home.

When Talia started to open her mouth, he shook his head and put a finger to his lips. With their eyes locked, she reached out and grabbed his hand. He instantly wanted to kick himself for not paying attention. He had to blame the ache in his back—otherwise, he never would have touched her. And she wouldn't want to relive his memories. Kirin didn't know how powerful she was or whether he could block her ability, but either way, he couldn't react in time when her soft hand came in contact with his. He felt a rush of electricity followed by his mind emptying into hers.

He didn't think it would be possible to watch the last three centuries blink by within seconds. She had a glimpse of everything that had happened in his life —the good, the bad, and the stuff no one should ever see. When she let go of his hand, a wave of emptiness flowed through his veins.

He wanted to reach out and grab her hand again, but not knowing what might happen, he murmured, "Kitchen. Now."

Talia grabbed a pair of gloves from her back pocket and put them on. Kirin opened his arms, gesturing for her to go first, then followed her down the hall. Talia immediately went to the other side of the counter—she must have wanted to put distance between them. After reviewing his own life, he understood the feeling. He didn't tell her he could jump over the counter and cuff her within seconds.

Mmm, cuffs, his dragon purred. Kirin chose to ignore his dragon and sat on the stool in front of Talia. A tiredness he had never experienced before came over him. He didn't understand it. He was a dragon shifter and was untouchable. He never worried about being weak, but at the moment, he could barely function. He struggled to process what had happened.

He studied the woman. "What did you see?" he asked quietly.

She licked her lips as though attempting to buy herself some time. "Everything. In one wild whoosh."

He nodded. "Is that normal?"

She shook her head. "This has never happened to me before."

Kirin scrutinized her for some sign that she was judging him, but she simply bit her cheek.

"Talia, say what you have to say."

She inhaled deeply. "What's going to happen to us?"

He leaned back and stared at his hands. "I don't know. I'm supposed to turn you in. Then the council..."

She walked around the counter and stood in front of him. "No. If you don't turn us in, I mean." She stood there, wringing her hands.

"And why would I do that?" He frowned, and for the first time since he'd arrived, Kirin was nervous.

"She didn't do it."

It was the same song and dance almost every one

of his charges had said. "If she didn't do it, let's go talk to Gideon and explain what happened."

Talia threw her hands up and paced back and forth in the small kitchen. He couldn't help but stare at her ass. She was sexy, and something about her drew his instincts out. He wanted to help her, but he also had a duty to the council and a mountain he needed to fill with gold.

"Gideon wants a name, and I can't give him that," she said.

"What can you give him?"

She leveled her tired brown eyes on him. "The same thing I told him in the warehouse. She didn't do it. No, I can't seem to lock in on who killed her parents. But if you'd seen her with her parents, you would understand."

There's nothing in the case notes about Talia and Alida knowing each other.

She must have realized where Kirin's thoughts had gone, because she said, "No, I never met her family before. But I touched her, and the memories of her with her parents floated through me. They didn't want anyone finding out about her powers. Her parents worried on her first day of school that she would accidentally use them."

Kirin pinched the bridge of his nose. "Gideon

said she didn't have powers. But that's a lie. I witnessed her disappearing in front of my eyes. And I'm guessing that she has more powers than transportation."

Talia glanced down the hallway. "Her powers don't matter. Proving she is innocent is the only thing I care about. And you will not say anything about what you saw her do."

Kirin didn't understand why it bothered him that she wouldn't tell him what the girl's other powers were. It wasn't as if they would be in his life after that day. Maybe if he gained a little more trust, she would open up more. "What did you see when you touched my hand?"

"Your whole life."

"I'm really old. Are you sure your vision showed my whole life? I highly doubt you would sit next to me if you'd witnessed the things I did."

"I didn't only get the images—I also received how you felt during each one. Those men who killed your dad deserved what you did. I'm not here to judge you. I want to protect Alida."

He didn't know how comfortable he was with her seeing so much of his past. For some reason, he wanted to hide the evils of the world from her. "You are adamant that the girl is innocent. I need more. Tell me everything from the top."

"When I touched the knife at the council, I saw Alida pick it up. But her parents were already dead, and she didn't have any blood on her clothes. How could she do such a brutal murder, and how did the council show up minutes after?"

"Maybe she showered and came back downstairs to clean up the mess." Kirin knew when the words came out of his mouth that they sounded stupid. He blamed it on exhaustion from reliving his life in the blink of an eye.

Talia scoffed at his comment. "You really think an eight-year-old brutally murdered her parents, walked upstairs, took a shower, and then walked back down and started to clean up? You're wrong."

"I don't know what she did. But we need to meet with Gideon and figure out what is going on."

Talia crossed her arms, causing her boobs to become Kirin's focal point. "Like I said, I can prove her innocence. And my eyes are up here."

Kirin ignored her calling him out. "Now?"

She sighed. "Soon."

That wasn't going to help them. He had a job to do. He had never hesitated. Kirin had spent more time talking to her than he had with any other charge. He didn't have the luxury of caring whether the little girl was guilty. "You do realize that whether or not she's guilty, you are. You're charged with aiding and abetting."

She threw her hands in the air. "It's not like I had a choice. I touched her..."

He rubbed his forehead. "And she teleported?"

Talia nodded. "And took me with her. Please just give me more time."

He wasn't completely insensitive. *Didn't Kia describe me as a bunny rabbit?* He just needed to be in the right situation, around the right people. He needed someone who wouldn't take advantage of him. And since Talia needed him to give her a chance, this was not that situation.

"Can't do it," he said. "Let's get the girl. I'll hold your hand while I pick her up. And then we'll be on our way."

Talia grabbed a soda from the fridge. She didn't bother asking if he wanted something to drink. "Kael said you were a good guy and would help us. He made sure you were the one on our case. Seems like another council member doesn't know his ass from his mouth. All you want is a paycheck, don't—"

Kirin grabbed her arm and ignored the tingles. "What do you mean you talked to Kael? When?"

She looked back down the hall as if worried Alida would hear. "We had a mishap."

"I need more than that. Tell me what happened." *What the fuck is Kael trying to pull?*

"Alida accidentally"—Talia took a sip of her drink buying time—"transported us to Kael's office, and he showed up."

"He just let you go," Kirin said.

"Yes. He was friends with Alida's parents. He worked to get me and you on the case so we could prove her right."

Kirin had heard enough. Kael would have called him in that case. Talia was grasping at straws.

"Let's go get Alida." Kirin stood up. He was adamant, but Talia didn't budge. She was blocking him. He placed his hands on her biceps to move her to the side. She was so tiny he could lift her without even straining.

But at their at their touch, he froze. Something happened. He felt... something he couldn't express. This woman. She couldn't be. Kirin stared deep into her eyes. She stared right back and never flinched despite his golden dragon eyes. He'd found her—his mate. And she was a criminal wanted by the council for aiding and abetting. *Well, doesn't that just throw a wrench in the works.*

9

TALIA

"What was that?" Talia rubbed her forehead. When Kirin grabbed her arm, she expected to see more from his past. She didn't know if there was anything else left to view of his life. But her body hummed with electricity, and when he let go, she wanted to reach back out. She needed to stop herself from leaning toward him.

The only thing Talia had known about dragons was the information that poured the first time she touched Kirin. She racked her brain and found nothing that explained his dilated eyes or the electricity that coursed through her body. She didn't think it was possible, but his golden eyes almost glowed for a second. If she weren't staring directly into them, she would have missed it. He shook his head.

A million questions kept running through her head. *Why doesn't he say anything? Is he being coy?* No matter how sexy the muscular man was, her goal was to protect the little girl in the other room. Kirin stood between her and making sure the girl was safe. Maybe after she proved the girl's innocence, she could look at the good-looking mercenary. But right now wasn't the time to lust over him.

Talia had made up her mind. If he would not level with her, she didn't need him around. "Fine. I'll go grab Alida." *And run with her.* She didn't say the second part—the sexy man didn't need to know her plan.

Kirin stood in the kitchen with his arms crossed. "Are we going to talk about what just happened?" He looked a little too sure of himself.

"I don't know what you are talking about."

He raised one eyebrow. *How can one expression make me want to melt into his arms?*

"Is that how you want to play this?" He gestured between them.

The conversation was heading down a road she didn't want to go down at the moment. Kirin stepped forward and, before Talia could process anything, wrapped an arm around her and pulled her in close. He leaned down and pressed his lips to hers. It stunned her for a second, but then her body melted into his, as though he was calling to her. Everything that had gone wrong that day went away. The only thing on her mind was the warmth of his lips.

Kirin pulled her in closer, and his tongue swiped across her lips. She automatically opened, granting him entrance. The more he ran his hands down her back, the more she wanted to wrap her legs around him. She needed to focus her mind. He was still the enemy. Talia didn't know if he even planned to turn them in, but with his tongue in her mouth, they weren't solving the issues at hand.

Talia pressed her hands against Kirin's chest. She needed to stop the kiss. She pulled her head back and shoved Kirin away. His eyes glowing yellow, he reached up to pull her back.

"I don't know what happened, but that cannot—I repeat, *cannot*—happen again."

Kirin crossed his arms. "Don't you feel something between us?"

Does this guy understand what happened around him? "It doesn't matter what I feel," she said. "Alida is the only thing I need to think about."

"This will not go away. You can't keep ignoring it."

Talia huffed. "I've known you less than an hour. It's not like I have ignored you for weeks. You don't always get what you want. Now, let me go check on Alida." She slipped around Kirin, making sure not to touch him, and left the room before he could mutter a word or stop her. She couldn't talk about anything between them—a little girl in the other room depended on her.

As soon as she rounded the corner, she raced down the hall to Alida. Talia didn't know if her heart was pounding because of what she planned to do or because of the sexy man standing in the other room. Talia touched her mouth, remembering his soft lips.

She didn't try to be quiet but threw open the door, letting it crash against the wall. Alida sat up straight. Talia didn't have time to wonder if the sound would let Kirin know they planned to run. The little girl read Talia's face and wrapped her arms around herself, terrified.

Talia's only goal was to get them out of the room. She hoped Alida had slept long enough and her powers were strong enough to transport them out of her apartment. Talia ran toward the bed and Alida with her arms wide open. As if Alida completely understood what was to happen next, she stood up on the bed and launched herself into Talia's arms. The minute they connected, there was a flash of light, and the room disappeared, but not before they saw the mercenary standing in the doorway, shaking his head at them. He wore a smirk, which bothered her. *Why would he be smirking?*

When Talia opened her eyes again, they were in her grandparents' mountain cabin. It had popped into her mind as she ran toward Alida. She shivered. The cabin had been empty for years. When her grandparents passed away, they gave the cabin to Talia. The cabin had too many memories of her parents, and she couldn't bring herself to go there. One good thing about the cabin was that no one knew she had it or that her grandparents had ever owned it. Talia didn't know why she hadn't thought to go there earlier.

She grinned at Alida, who still had her arms around Talia's neck. "You did it." Talia walked toward the couch and pulled off the sheet. It worried her that when she leaned down, Alida didn't release her arms. "You're safe here. Let me start a fire."

The little girl let go of her neck. "I'm scared."

"You're safe here—I promise."

Alida nodded, though she didn't seem to believe Talia's words.

Talia glanced around the cabin. They were in the center of the main room. The place was dusty, which made sense because no one in the family had used the place in years.

"You're exhausted, little one," Talia murmured. "Let's go to bed, and we'll talk more when we wake up."

A few candles and matches were laid on the coffee table. Talia leaned forward and lit two candles, one for Alida and the other so Talia wouldn't fall as she went to get bedding. Talia walked down the hall to the bedroom to grab a few blankets and pillows from the closet. She planned to set up their beds in front of the fireplace. The light from the candle in her hand flickered. A photo on the wall caught her attention before she made it to the closet. She held the candle to the picture to get a better look. It was a picture of her parents and Kael. *How did I never notice that before? Why did he act like he had no clue who I was when we first met?* Talia pulled the frame off the wall and took the picture out. She wanted to save it for later and confront Kael.

The door to the bedroom squeaked as she opened it. Talia held the candle up, and the room was illuminated. Her breath hitched as her eyes landed on another picture of her parents. This one was their wedding. Kael stood next to her dad, and both men were laughing. *What the fuck is going on?*

Alida called her name from the living room. Talia glanced at the photo one more time and called, "I'll be back in a second." She walked to the closet and opened the wood door, revealing a stack of warm quilts. She pulled out a quilt and held it under one arm then grabbed a couple of pillows off the bed.

When she walked back into the living room. Alida jumped off the couch and snatched the blanket from her hand. The girl reached up and took her free hand. Talia's heart melted. She didn't know if she could ever let Alida go when they proved her innocence. The little girl had wormed her way into Talia's heart. Talia was determined not to let her out of her sight.

They worked together to lay the pillows and blanket out in front of the fireplace. Once Talia had Alida tucked in under the covers, she took the light and walked to the den area. That was where her grandfather kept the wood to build a fire. Talia hoped a few pieces would still be there. She didn't want to go out into the wintery night and chop wood. When her eyes landed on a nice pile of wood, Talia let out a sigh of relief. Things were starting to look up.

With firewood in her arms, she headed back to the living room to find Alida almost asleep. Talia worked to get the fire started, but the matches were old and not catching. Talia leaned back and mumbled, "Fuck."

Alida giggled. "Let me help."

Before Talia could ask how she would help, the young girl sat up and closed her eyes, and seconds later, the paper Talia had put in the fireplace came alive with flames.

"How?"

Alida shrugged her little shoulders. "I thought about fire and paper, and it happened."

"Have you done this before?"

Talia had never met someone with this much power. Her heart broke a little as she thought about how much Alida would need to hide from the world. The council would use her if they ever found out what she could do. But Talia felt confident they were safe in the cabin. No one knew about this place. No one would remember to check here. Hell, she'd half forgotten it existed until the minute she needed a place.

The fire roared, and warmth filled the room. She just didn't know what she would do about food. They couldn't chance going to a store—she knew better than to do anything that might give her location away.

"That was my first time," Alida said.

Talia had been so deep in her thoughts that she'd forgotten she'd asked Alida a question.

"I just had a feeling, and then I did it. Mom and Dad always said I would have magic beyond anyone's belief. What will Gideon do once he finds me?"

Talia wanted to promise that Gideon would never find her, but Talia didn't know if she could keep that promise, and she didn't plan to lie to Alida. "I'm going to do everything in my power to keep you safe."

Alida looked off into space for a second. "That man will find us again," she announced as she cuddled closer.

Talia's body warmed at the mention of Kirin. "No, he won't, sweet girl. We're safe here." Talia wanted to believe her own words, but Alida had yet to be wrong.

"He will be here before morning."

10

KIRIN

He chuckled when he found himself alone in Talia's apartment. Sure, he could rush off and try to find her again, but it might make more sense to explore her apartment and look for a hint of where she might be. So he made his way to the bathroom. He looked through her medicine cabinet. She didn't seem to be on any meds. For some reason, that mattered.

HE MOVED BACK to her bedroom. He wandered into the closet and pulled out a weekender bag. Then he went back to her dresser and started pulling out socks and underwear. He grabbed shirts, jeans, and a pair of sneakers. He grabbed her a warmer coat. She'd need that in the mountains.

WHEN SHE'D TOUCHED HIM, he couldn't wait to wrap her in his arms. And when their lips touched, he felt something familiar he couldn't put his finger on it. His dragon hummed, telling him to head up the mountain. Kirin knew where Talia was. *How do I know?*

Kirin didn't understand why his dragon knew how to find Talia, but his brother Kia might have some insight into that new ability—if not, he could find the information on the Internet. He reached in his pocket and called his brother. It rang a few times before Kirin heard his brother's voice.

"DUDE, it's after midnight. What do you want now?" Kia grumbled.

"FINDING YOUR MATE... what happens? What kind of connection is there?" His mind was racing. He couldn't believe it had taken him this long to figure out Talia was his mate. His dragon grumbled that he'd known all along. And then it hit him that the woman from his dreams was her. He didn't need to see the face of the woman he'd dreamt about—he knew it was her.

"You do realize you're the big brother," Kia mumbled. "You're the one who's supposed to know all this and tell the rest of us, dumbass. Why didn't you call Mom?"

"I didn't think I would ever find my mate, so I never looked. You know why I didn't call Mom. Now, tell me what you know."

"Do I sound like I know a damn thing about women, let alone finding a mate? No one has been more single than me through the years."

"You are the only one who is computer savvy."

· · ·

"Do you really think you can google what happens when a dragon finds his mate? You're the one with all of the family books. Why are you calling me instead of looking it up?"

Kirin pinched the bridge of his nose. "It doesn't matter why I need you to find the information. I need your help, please."

"Fuck, I'm sorry, man. Give me a second to see what I can find." Kirin could hear Kia typing on his laptop. Kirin spotted a pink suitcase in the corner. He wondered what his place would look like with pink all over. He knew he would let Talia decorate it how she wanted. His place screamed bachelor. Alida could move in with them, because from this moment forward, he would do everything to protect them both. His dragon would never let Talia go, and he knew Talia would never let the little girl go.

Kia's voice came back over the phone. "I don't know, man. You know just about everything on the Internet about shifters is made up. It's not like a wolf shifter would actually leave info about what it's like when he finds his mate. Dragon shifters are far more rare. There's nothing." He was quiet for a moment. "Wait. Did you find your mate? What the hell is going on?"

KIRIN GROANED. "I don't know how to explain it. So, I met someone. I stared at her. And now... I know where she is... at all times."

"SO THE WOMAN you are going to turn over to the council is your mate. How does your dragon feel about turning her in?" Kia could barely get the words out of his mouth, he was laughing so hard. "Wait, we need to conference Conley in."

"NO. Conley doesn't need to hear about this. And we both know he knows jack about finding his mate." Conley had a different woman each night and never wanted to settle down. "And furthermore, I'm not going to turn her in." Nope, she was going to be added to his hoard, and he would never let her go.

· · ·

"IF I FIND ANYTHING, I will call you. If you need me to help, just say the word."

"THANKS, bro. Don't tell Mom either." Kirin clicked off the phone.

WHEN HE WALKED BACK to his bike, he saw the nosy neighbor poking her head out the window. He lifted his hand and waved. A chuckle escaped him when the old lady waved back. She didn't care that she'd been caught staring. He wondered what someone her age was still doing up. He would ask Talia what she was. Talia seemed to attract rare supernatural beings.

KIRIN PLACED Talia's bag on the back of his bike and grabbed the rope from his saddlebags. He pointed his bike in the direction of his house. He would need to grab clothes for himself and food for everyone. He didn't think Talia and Alida would have any food where they'd gone.

· · ·

WHEN HE ARRIVED at his house, his phone vibrated in his pocket. Kirin hoped it was his brother with more information. His brow furrowed at the unknown number of whomever was calling at midnight.

"YES?" he barked into the phone.

"HAVE YOU FOUND THEM?"

Kirin ground his teeth at the sound of Kael's voice. He rubbed between his eyes. "I will bring them in." Maybe Talia hadn't lied to him earlier. He wasn't about to play all of his cards.

KAEL WAS silent for a few seconds. "Hmm."

"WHAT DO YOU MEAN 'HMM'?"

"Do you think the girl did it?"

·   ·   ·

KIRIN PULLED the phone back and stared at it. He wasn't sure what Kael was pulling. "What's going on?"

"I DON'T KNOW if I can trust you."

"IT'S the fucking middle of the night. Spit it out, Kael."

KAEL LET OUT A SIGH. "Alida is important to me."

KIRIN'S HEADED STARTED to throb even more. "Then why did you let Gideon take her in and act like she killed her parents? We both know she didn't do it." There was no point in keeping anything from Kael.

"GIDEON DIDN'T KNOW I was friends with her family, and I'm trying to figure out what he is up to. I need him to think I'm on his side."

· · ·

"You could have told me this hours ago."

Kirin could hear Kael breathing hard, probably pacing. "I figured you would have them by now and Talia would persuade you. Also, I heard a wizard might be after you."

"Really? You're going to casually say 'Hey, someone is after you because you killed a council member from another state'? Also, it's hard to catch someone when they keep transporting the second you find them." Kirin let out a sigh. "Stop fucking laughing."

"I can just picture the big bad Kirin showing up and an eight-year-old slipping through his grasp. And sorry about that wizard. I'm in contact with the council, but keep an eye out. Also, you need to grab Alida's medication. The longer she is without it, the more her powers will grow. We don't know what she will be able to do."

. . .

GREAT. His mate was with a girl who didn't know how to control her powers. "What is Alida to you?"

"I WAS REALLY close with her parents."

"WILL YOU TAKE HER?" He needed to know what he was up against. Kirin had a feeling if Talia had to give up Alida, it would crush her, and Kirin would do anything to make his mate happy. If that meant he had to kill Kael, so be it.

"IF YOU ARE WORRIED I would take her from Talia, no. I saw the way Talia looked at her when they appeared in my office. I sent Alida a message to trust Talia."

THIS SHIT KEPT GETTING STRANGER. "You can communicate with Alida?"

"YES, I CAN SEND HER MESSAGES."

. . .

"TELL her I'm coming for them, and I won't hurt either of them. I will work to prove Alida is innocent."

KIRIN GRABBED his go-bag from the closet and headed down to the kitchen.

"THANK YOU. And, Kirin—be safe. The Virginia council is mad you brought Zyra in."

KIRIN CLICKED OFF THE PHONE. He cleaned out his fridge and grabbed cookies from the pantry for Alida. His next stop was Alida's house, only this time, in addition to packing the little girl's clothes, he grabbed a couple of toys from the bed and her pink blanket. He scoffed at the tablet on the night-stand but grabbed it anyway along with two books. When he was about to zip up the bag, he heard the door downstairs creak open.

HE LET his dragon come forward to sense who had

entered the house. The stranger was stomping around. Kirin slowly stepped out of the room and walked down the stairs. The intruder was in the office. When he rounded the corner, he saw a man sitting at the computer. *Fuck.* It was another hired mercenary—a crappy one. Jeremiah was sloppy and frequently killed his charges instead of bringing them in for justice. He couldn't let Jeremiah get anywhere near Talia and Alida.

"WHAT ARE YOU DOING HERE, JEREMIAH?"

THE FUCKER JUMPED to his feet. "This one is mine. Stay away, Kirin. I wouldn't want to have to kill Gideon's favorite."

HIS FINGERS ITCHED to pull the gun out of his waistband. Kirin didn't like to kill with bullets, but it wasn't always easy to shift in a house since his dragon was the same size and usually destroyed whatever building it was in. Jeremiah rounded the desk and reached for his belt.

.   .   .

"FUCK," Kirin mumbled as he grabbed his gun and sent two bullets hitting Jeremiah, one in each leg, making Jeremiah scream. "I told you to leave it alone. You can have my next three cases. Drop this one." When it didn't look like he would, Kirin said, "If you don't drop this case, I will burn your pack and eat the ashes of the dead."

JEREMIAH'S WOLF snarled at him. "Pay me five grand, and I will drop it." Kirin reached into his pocket and threw the money on the ground. "Make sure to clean up your blood on the way out." He turned on his heel and grabbed Alida's case file.

JEREMIAH WOULD BE FINE—HIS wolf would heal him. But Kirin didn't believe for one moment the wolf would stop, so he reached into his pocket and called the alpha.

"YOU'D BETTER HAVE a good reason to be calling me in the middle of the night, Kirin."

· · ·

"DON'T GROWL AT ME. Call your wolf off of the case he's on."

"I'M NOT CALLING him off if Gideon told him to do something. You know I don't have a say."

KIRIN WALKED TOWARD HIS TRUCK. "I will owe you. And if something happens to Talia, I will burn your pack."

"DON'T THREATEN MY PEOPLE."

"WELL, one of my people is being threatened."

"FUCK. I will call him off. But you'd better come when I call in that favor. You owe the pack."

"THANKS. Oh, and you might want to send someone. Jeremiah has a couple of bullet holes in his legs."

Not waiting for an answer, Kirin hung up and slipped his phone into his pocket.

KIRIN DIDN'T NEED an address to Talia's cabin—it was more like a pull. With each turn, his dragon wanted him to drive faster. He drove through the mountains, and when he almost passed a hidden gravel road with overgrown trees, he could feel her close. Kirin turned off his headlights and drove down the unkempt road. It looked like no one had been there in years. When the trees cleared, there sat a small cabin. The place looked dark, but he knew they were inside. He parked then grabbed the suitcases and the box of food.

HE SHOOK his head and opened the cabin door with a twist of the knob. Kirin couldn't help but stop and stare at the sight of Talia and Alida curled up in front of the fire.

KIRIN PUT the suitcases down and headed toward the kitchen. It was dark, but he didn't need light to see.

He set the box down on the counter and started to unpack the food.

Hearing the shift in Talia's breathing, he knew she'd woken up. He looked in her direction, and their eyes met. She didn't look surprised to see him. Talia got up and padded across the living room. She raised her eyebrow.

"I FIGURED you would be hungry. I also brought clothes for you and Alida." He reached into his pocket and pulled out Alida's meds. "Kael said Alida might need these."

TALIA OPENED HER MOUTH, but just then, a loud crash came from outside. Talia went running toward Alida. Kirin reached out and grabbed her arm.

"LET me go check it out. If I'm not back in ten minutes, you guys need to go. I will find you again."

"BUT IT MIGHT NOT BE SAFE."

·   ·   ·

KIRIN LEANED DOWN and placed a kiss on Talia's forehead. "Ten minutes."

11

TALIA

Her forehead tingled where he'd placed the kiss. At first, when she saw him, she felt calm, peaceful even. Then she remembered that this guy was going to take her and Alida to the council. The young girl had warned her Kirin would show up, but for some reason, Alida didn't seem scared about the mercenary finding them. When Talia walked over to the kitchen and saw him putting groceries away, the worry dissipated a little.

Talia could only hope Kirin had changed his mind about turning them in. Gideon would probably see to it that she never saw the light of day again. He'd make sure someone killed her and Alida, and she didn't even know why. *What could he possibly have against this little girl?*

She looked at the door Kirin had walked out of two minutes and thirty seconds earlier. He'd told her to wait ten minutes, and she would do that, but not a second longer. Alida was her first priority. Needing something to do, she walked back into the kitchen and looked at the items Kirin had brought. The hot cocoa caught her eye. She used the long wooden matches to light the stove. Talia poured some of the milk Kirin had brought and rested it on the burner. Hot cocoa solved all the problems in the world for a few seconds. While she was stirring the pot of milk, a bright light flashed through the window, almost blinding her.

Talia rushed toward the door and grabbed the bat beside it. It would have to do. With a Louisville slugger in one hand, she reached for the front door and twisted the doorknob. She knew she should run to Alida and get her out of there, but something deep down pulled for her to go and check on Kirin. She didn't want to see him hurt.

A blast of cold winter air hit her as the door opened. The fresh snow crunched under her boot as she walked down the stairs of the cabin. A grunt came from the side of the house, followed by another bright flash. She had to shield her eyes.

The contrast from dark to bright blinded her for a second. The sound of a moan had her walking faster. When she turned the corner, she found Kirin standing with a knife drawn. He had not only a weapon, but he was also more substantial. Somehow, he had doubled in size, and his fingers had turned to talons.

"Leave, warlock. Your beef is not with me." Kirin's voice was gravelly and hard to make out.

The man in dark robes crouched down, holding his hands in front of him. "You killed my brother." Another shot of bright light exploded from the wizard's hands. Kirin dove to the side to escape what looked like a lightning bolt. The magic missed Kirin and hit the tree behind him.

"I didn't kill your brother. Gideon asked me to bring him in."

Light sparked from his fingers. "Gideon said you killed him."

Kirin ran a hand down his face. "I didn't kill your brother. I delivered him to Gideon two days ago. Ask Kael. He was there when I brought him in."

"Are you saying your council leader is lying?"

"Clearly, since I didn't kill your brother." Kirin seemed to be frustrated with the wizard.

The wizard let another lightning bolt from his fingers. Kirin moved at the speed of light and rolled to the side, missing the attack. The magic hit another tree and caused it to fall down. Kirin jumped back to his feet. The wizard was in front of Kirin and placed his hands around his neck. Talia couldn't watch some warlock try to kill Kirin. She trudged through the snow with the bat in her hands.

When Kirin caught sight of her, he shook his head. *Silly man.* She would protect him from the angry warlock. She raised the bat, and before she could swing it, the warlock dropped his hands from Kirin and shoved her with enough force to throw her ten feet away. The fluffy snow protected her ass when she hit the ground. Her head wasn't as lucky, as it hit a tree.

Black seeped into her vision, but the load roar brought her back to the present. Talia watched as Kirin closed his eyes and chanted. In the blink of an eye, a dragon stood where Kirin had been a moment before. The dragon was taller than the cabin, and when he extended his gold wings, his body took up the yard. The gold of the dragon shimmered in the night. Talia was mesmerized. The dragon's red eyes homed in on her.

The warlock must not have realized a big-ass dragon had appeared behind him. "How dare you stop me from killing my brother's killer?"

Why does he have to be so dramatic? Kirin said he didn't do it. But the wizard didn't seem to care. He raised his arms up and sent a lightning bolt in Talia's direction.

The massive dragon leaped between her and the bolt of magic and spread his wings. Talia knew if it had hit her, she would have died. The dragon grunted with pain when the bolt hit his wing. Her eyes locked onto the dragon's before he turned toward the wizard. He was angry. A snarl ripped from his throat. Kirin let out a stream of fire at the warlock. The warlock screamed and vanished.

Kirin had singed all the trees near the cabin. Talia took stock of the cabin and let out a sigh. He hadn't burned it down. The dragon took a step toward her. His weight shook the ground. She should have been scared of the massive creature.

"Can I touch you?" she asked.

Kirin let out a huff and nodded. She couldn't help giggling. Talia slowly got up from the ground. She reached out and ran her hands over the gold scales. The urge to take off her gloves was over-whelming. In all of her years of touching objects, she'd normally tried to stay away from things, not knowing what she would see. Talia worked her gloves off, and with one touch, she was transported into a vision.

The sun shone down on them. Talia and Alida sat on the dragon's back as he flew through the mountains. Giggles erupted from Alida as he swooped down to the tree line. Talia pulled back her hand to stop the vision. She had never seen the future, but she didn't have time to process what this meant because the dragon before her disappeared, replaced by Kirin. A very naked Kirin. She trailed her eyes down his body and got stuck on his hard abs. She was about to continue the journey down when she noticed that his side was red and blistered.

"You're hurt."

Kirin shrugged. "He hit me with a lightning bolt."

Talia ran as fast as she could through the snow to Kirin. The ugly red mark down his side was a reminder of how he'd saved her life.

"Why?" She couldn't understand why he'd saved her. It would have been easier to take Alida in if she was dead.

Kirin reached forward and tucked her blond hair behind her ear. "I will always protect you." When he pulled his arm back, he winced.

"Come on. Let's get you inside and fix the wound on your side." Talia didn't give him time to respond. She grabbed his hand and dragged him toward the cabin. She peeked inside. Alida was still curled up by the fire, sleeping. She didn't want to disturb the girl, so she grabbed a candle off the table and pulled Kirin toward the bedroom. "Sit."

Talia walked into the bathroom and grabbed the first aid kit. When she returned, Kirin had put on a pair of workout shorts. That would make it a little easier to work on the sexy dragon. Talia spread antiseptic along the red skin. Kirin winced under her touch.

"Sorry," she mumbled.

"I like your hands on me. You know, my dragon will heal this in an hour."

She knew that, but for some reason, she felt like she needed to take care of him. "Let me do this."

"What did you see when you touched my dragon?"

Talia licked her lips. "I saw the future."

Kirin's eyes glowed bright yellow. His dragon had come to the surface to find out what she had to say.

"How do you know it was the future? And what was it?"

Talia put the cap back on the medicine. "Alida and I were flying in the sky with a gold dragon."

"Hmm."

She didn't want to talk about it anymore. "I'm going to go check on the hot chocolate. You can rest in here." Her body was on fire being so close to the sexy man. She needed to step away for two minutes. Talia walked down the hall. She could hear steps behind her. The stubborn dragon hadn't listened to her about lying down.

The hot milk was simmering on the stove with the burner low enough that the milk didn't get over-cooked. She poured two cups.

"Why is that man after you, and do we need to leave?" Talia passed him a mug of hot chocolate.

Kirin took a sip of the cocoa. "He won't be back for a few days. I burned him pretty bad."

"Did you kill his brother?"

One side of Kirin's lip turned down. "No. I turned his brother over to Gideon a couple of days ago for trial."

Talia spun the cup in her hands. "It seems Gideon has been up to no good lately." But she wondered if it was more than that.

Kirin rested his elbows on the counter. "I've spent years doing what he said and never looked into any of the cases. Fuck, he's the head of the council. But something is not right."

She would protect the girl. "I'm not letting anything happen to Alida."

"You need to protect yourself and Alida. Next time, grab her and leave. I can handle a warlock on my own."

"She needs to sleep. I'm not sure if she can teleport anywhere. I haven't been able to feed her. Are you planning to turn us in?" Talia needed to figure out what his plan was.

"I'm not turning you in," he murmured.

That didn't make her feel any better. "What changed? What's different?" She shook her head. She'd never learned to trust easily. In fact, the psychic abilities made it more challenging for her to even relax with people. She'd warmed to wearing gloves, and it helped some but not entirely. And now she was so tired she could cry. She was already tired of running. She wanted to believe him, but she couldn't. Not yet.

Kirin licked his lips. "I don't know how to explain this. I don't understand it either." He shook his head. "I can't turn you in. I can't let anything happen to you. My dragon wanted to eat the warlock for even trying to hurt you. I didn't have control once I shifted, and that's never happened before."

"That wasn't the case a couple of hours ago."

He moved closer to her and held out his hand. Talia took a deep breath. If he was letting her touch him, he obviously wanted her to see something.

"Don't you even want to know how I ended up here?" He held out his hand. "Take it."

Talia reached out and took his hand. She could see so much of his life this way. She saw that he had two brothers. Talia saw that he did his job and was good at it. She saw him watching the report on her and Alida. She could feel him softening even then. And finally, she saw the moment he grabbed her arm. Her skin was covered by her jacket, which was why she had seen none of this before.

She released him quickly as if the touch had burned her. She believed him. Talia didn't understand it, but she knew he wouldn't turn her in. Somehow, she was safe with him. And that was what she would tell Alida when the little girl woke up. She picked up the hot chocolate in both hands and sipped it while considering what she'd seen. She couldn't take her eyes off Kirin. "What now?"

"Well, you said you thought you could prove Alida was innocent. I say we work on that."

"We?" she asked, her brows arched.

He nodded. "We. And get used to it. We're going to be *we* for a very long time."

12

KIRIN

He was doing everything wrong. He needed to tell her she was his mate. But he still hadn't wrapped his mind around having found her. There was something about this woman that made him mess up. He couldn't pull off his usual air of indifference around her because... he cared, dammit. Kirin cared about her. He cared about everything she cared about. And it was utterly screwing him up.

Kirin groaned. "I'm sorry."

She frowned. "For what? Almost getting me killed earlier? I'm still alive." She smiled, and instantly, his heart thumped harder in his chest.

"I will make sure he dies next time." His smile

quickly faded when he saw her eyeing him curiously.

"You don't smile much. In fact, in not one of the trillion memories that flashed before my eyes did you ever smile. What's going on?"

He shook his head. He couldn't tell her. She wasn't ready to hear that they would be together forever because his dragon had chosen her.

"Let's focus on Alida. Let's work on saving her. And we'll save you by default." He reached out and laid a hand on her arm because he couldn't help himself. "We'll fix this. We'll make this right. I promise." He swallowed hard. Thinking about the potential loss of Talia made him more emotional than he'd ever been.

As if her name had summoned her, Alida walked into the kitchen, rubbing her eyes. "About time you got here."

Kirin couldn't hold back the chuckle. "You knew I would come? Why did you stay?"

The little girl rolled her eyes. "Kael said you would come."

Talia stopped making the sandwich she was working on. "When did you talk to Kael?"

Alida ducked her head. "I'm sorry. I used my powers."

"It's okay. Kael told me he would talk to you. I also brought your medicine. Do you want to take it?" Kirin felt like it was her choice.

"No, not yet." Her eyes glazed over for a second. If he hadn't been watching her so closely, he would have missed it. "Bad men will come."

Talia cleared her throat. "Here, you need to eat this. Let's go sit in the living room."

Kirin watched as the two people most important to him walked to the living room. He sat in silence and wondered how his life had changed so much in less than twelve hours. Alida and Talia giggled on the couch. The sound made his dragon happy. The fucker was flying around in his mind. He wanted Kirin to throw Talia over his shoulder and claim her.

Kirin sat next to Talia. Alida climbed off her side of the couch and onto his lap. It stunned him for a second before the young girl reached up and patted his face. "You will protect us." Then she went back to eating her sandwich.

Talia curled up next to him. He needed them to rest—he knew they would have a fight coming soon. He would need to contact his brothers. Kirin would do anything to protect these two. Once Alida finished eating, she curled up in his arms. It only took seconds before she fell back to sleep.

Talia smiled up at him. "She's precious, isn't she?" She had so much love in her eyes.

"Yes, and so are you."

A light blush spread across Talia's cheeks. She laid her head down on his shoulder and relaxed. She began to slide down the back of the sofa and finally landed in his arms. Then, and only then, was he able to sleep. While he slept, he dreamed. Usually, memories of the death of his dad or the woman he could never make out assaulted him when he slept. But this time, he was met with hopes for the future. At least, that was how he processed them. He saw him and Talia together, happy and surrounded by children. Alida was in the center of the children, acting like a big sister. He saw a big life, more significant than he ever dreamed of.

When he woke, which happened far later than normal, he realized that both Alida and Talia were awake with him on the couch, but neither had moved. They were simply lying there, watching him.

"Are you ready?" Alida asked.

"For what?" He tilted his head, wondering what she had in mind.

"We need to find the dark man," Alida said.

Kirin looked at Talia questioningly.

"The man who killed her parents. All she sees is a dark man."

It felt like a riddle. *What does that mean?* "Skin color?" He glanced back and forth between them.

Alida shook her head. "No. His spirit. He's a bad man. I didn't see him."

Talia looked at Kirin seriously. "We need to get back to the house. I need to feel the place out."

He nodded and cringed. The fight he'd had earlier had broken a bunch of items. He didn't like the idea. It was dangerous for both of them. There could be another mercenary waiting to see if they would return.

"How about I go and bring stuff back?" he asked.

"We have to go together," Alida said with confidence.

Kirin raised an eyebrow at Talia, and she shrugged.

"I don't want anything to happen to you," Kirin said.

She giggled in his arms. "Silly. We are here to help you. You can't do this on your own."

His dragon huffed at the girl's words. They had worked alone for years. And if Gideon felt like he was taking too long, he'd call in another mercenary, one who wouldn't feel any ties to Talia and wouldn't care about hurting a little girl. Then the complications would only grow.

He decided to call in to the council and buy them some time. He stood and motioned for Talia and Alida to be silent while he made his call to Gideon.

"Yes," Gideon answered.

"I found them. I'm working on bringing them in. They are a little tougher than I expected. Although, I suspect you knew this when you contacted me."

Gideon growled. "How much longer?"

"I don't know. I'm hoping to sneak in when they're asleep. So... maybe tonight? Early tomorrow?"

"I'll wait as long as I can, but you know how this works. You're the one who I called in as the A team," Gideon reminded him.

Kirin sighed. "I know." He wanted to call Gideon out on the fact that he'd already called on another mercenary.

Talia had her arms wrapped around Alida but kept her eyes on him during the conversation. Alida played with the blanket. He couldn't help studying her. *How can someone so young have so much power?* He wondered what her future held. He would do anything to protect her. As if reading his thoughts, she looked up from the blanket and smiled.

Talia looked back and forth between the two. "Alida, did you read Kirin's mind?"

The little girl shrugged. "I'm not saying I did, but if I did, I bet he wants to protect us. And he has some information to explain in the future."

Kirin was speechless. Each moment, he found out about another one of the girl's powers. The more he found out the more he wanted to protect her from the world. The flames in the fire had started to die down. Needing a second to comprehend what he'd found out and how he would protect them, Kirin grabbed a couple of logs and added them to the fire.

"Okay, Alida, I don't always have the best thoughts. Let's try not to read mine."

"Okay, but you were thinking really hard, and sometimes it's hard not to hear them. Like when Talia saw you without a shirt."

Talia's face turned bright red, and her mouth dropped open.

Kirin let out a chuckle. "I wouldn't mind hearing what Talia thought.

Talia put a hand over Alida's mouth. "That is none of your business."

Alida let out a giggle before her eyes glazed over. She went still, and Talia looked in Kirin's direction in a panic. This had to be related to one of her gifts, and she had to come out of it on her own. Kirin started to wonder if they would be better off giving the girl her pills. He worried that the amount of magic she kept performing would drain the young girl.

Kirin reached up and grabbed Talia's hand while they waited for the trance to end. Alida blinked, refocusing on the room. "Kael said Gideon has called more people to come after us. Kael has worked to send them in a redirection. He doesn't think anyone knows about the cabin."

It was nice that Kael gave them updates, but Kirin didn't want him to keep using the young girl. He stayed crouched in front of Alida. "Can you block Kael from communicating with you?"

Alida cocked her head in confusion. "Why?"

"I don't want you to get to run-down. You've used a lot of your powers lately, and Kael said you hadn't used them in a while."

Alida reached forward and grabbed his hand. "Don't worry, I'm fine. It will all work out."

The hairs on the back of Kirin's neck stood up. *Someone is here.* "Wait here. I will be right back."

"I'm coming with you," Talia said.

"No. Stay inside."

Kirin grabbed a shirt and threw it on before he walked out into the blistering cold. The temperature barely affected him, but he put the shirt on so he didn't meet his guest shirtless.

He let out an aggravated sigh when his eyes landed on the warlock from the night before. He'd brought someone else with him. Kirin stomped down the snow-covered steps. When he got to the bottom, he stood with his arms crossed and waited for the intruders to speak. He didn't have time to deal with these fuckers.

"We came to help you."

Kirin raised his brow and waited for the intruder to continue. The new warlock wore the same long blue robes as the other. They were both well over six feet tall. He had to guess they were brothers. They both had blond hair and blue eyes and looked similar.

"Help with what? I already told you I didn't kill your brother, but you attacked my mate."

The warlock's eyes widened for a second before he schooled his features. "It's come to our attention you weren't lying."

"Really. Attacking me two times and me telling

you wasn't enough?"

The new warlock crossed his arms. "Someone close to us lied. We wanted to let you know we are going to take care of that. We also came to help you with your mission."

"I don't need help." There is no way he would trust the men standing in front of him.

The one he'd burned earlier threw his arms up. Kirin caught a glimpse of scorched skin when his robe rose. Kirin's dragon smiled at seeing the man who'd dared touch their mate. He wanted to eat the fucker, but Kirin didn't have time to deal with that.

"Here. This might help you." The warlock held up a folder.

Kirin walked over and grabbed it from his hands. "Why are you giving this to me?"

"Our council doesn't want to go to war with your council. You are our only hope of avenging our brother's death."

"What makes you think I'm after the person who killed your brother?"

The two brothers glanced at each other. "If you aren't, we will eventually get vengeance in our brother's name."

Before he could ask more questions about the folder, the two brothers disappeared. Kirin glanced at the folder in his hand before he started to walk toward the house. When his foot hit the first step, he heard a blood-curdling scream coming from inside the house.

13

TALIA

"It's only a spider, Talia," Alida spit out between fits of laughter.

The creature climbing across the floor was more than a spider. Talia stood on the old chair and glanced at her bat on the other side of the room. Alida started to walk toward the spider.

"Alida, get your ass off the floor."

"Mom said *ass* is a bad word."

Talia couldn't help but roll her eyes. "Bad words can be used in times of panic. This right here is one of those times. The only option we have is to light the house on fire and transport out."

"But it's not even poisonous, and it won't hurt us."

"We don't know that. Do you have powers to talk to the spider? Did he tell you he won't murder you or me?"

Alida rolled her eyes. "I didn't speak to the spider, but it's a wolf spider. They aren't poisonous. We learned about them in science class."

"You can't b—" Talia's words were cut off when Kirin threw open the door. His talons were extended, and his gold eyes glowed. "What's wrong?" The words came out gravelly and hard to understand.

"Spider," Talia whispered.

Alida giggled, and the half dragon, half Kirin blinked in her direction. Kirin shrank back to his normal human size and stomped through the house. "Where?" His voice had turned normal. His black hair was messy from the wind outside. The floor creaked under each step he took.

"There. I think we need to burn the house down." It was the only valid option.

Kirin shook his head and walked toward the creature.

"Don't kill it. It's not poisonous," Alida stated.

The man was already wrapped around the little girl's finger. He leaned down, picked up the spider, walked to the front door, and let the fucker go. Talia saw him put it outside, but she didn't plan on leaving the chair anytime soon. When Kirin noticed her still up there, he walked over and wrapped his arms around her and pulled her down from the chair.

"Are you sure there are no more?"

"I will protect you if we find another one. But we need to leave soon." Kirin mumbled against her skin.

She knew it was only a matter of time before their location was found. Gideon had probably called in everyone he had. If Talia gambled, she would bet Gideon had found out about Alida's powers and wanted her back. She would bet he planned to hide her away and use her for his gain. Talia didn't plan on that happening, and the sooner they got ready, the sooner she could be far away from the giant spider, who might decide to come back.

"Who was outside?"

Kirin ran his hand through his hair, and Talia noticed that he was holding a folder.

"The warlock from earlier and one of his brothers." Kirin leaned forward and silenced her next question with his lips.

The only reason she pulled back from his warm, soft lips was because she heard Alida say "Eww." When Talia pulled back, Kirin had a smile. God, she wanted to melt into a puddle when the man smiled. But they were working on borrowed time. She knew it. Kirin knew it. And there was a distinct possibility that Alida had figured it out.

She took a deep breath before stepping back from him. "Do we have to worry about the warlocks?"

"No, they gave us information. I was about to look at it when I heard you scream."

Talia ducked her head. "I need to get ready. Let's eat, and let's go." She looked at Kirin.

He nodded in agreement. "I'll feed Alida, and you can washup," Kirin said as he walked toward Alida and lifted her into the air.

That man knew how to make Talia melt. But instead of openly gawking at Kirin, she brushed past him and made her way down the hall. No one had been in the cabin for years, and she wondered if there was even anything there for her to use to get cleaned up.

Then she heard footsteps behind her. Kirin stood there, looking sheepish. "I forgot—I brought these for you." He passed her toiletry bag over.

She stared up into his face while she took the bag. "How did you know?"

He shrugged. "Common sense?"

Then he disappeared from the room, but not before laying a hand on her back. She wasn't sure whether the move was designed to comfort her or him, but she wasn't opposed to his touch, which surprised her.

Since they were in a rush, Talia made short work of taking a shower and getting dressed. While she cleaned up, she split her time between thinking through their game plan and listening for any signs of trouble in the kitchen. She made her way back to the living area, trying to keep her fear in order. Before Talia could enter the room, Kirin was there.

"What's bothering you?" He laid a hand on her back.

Her brow furrowed. "How did you know?"

He shrugged. "I just did."

"I'm worried we won't be able to prove her innocence." It was the first time Talia had said it out loud. With each second that they didn't prove Alida's innocence, it felt like they would never find the answer.

"Come on." Kirin tugged on her hand. "I have pancakes ready for you. We better hurry before Alida eats them all."

Talia sat down at the table next to Alida. The young girl was eating her pancakes. Talia took a bite of hers. It tasted like heaven. When she looked at Kirin, he had his head buried in the folder.

"Anything in the file?"

Kirin shut the folder and let out a sigh. "Nothing helpful. It's a list of all the council members who have gone missing over the past year. A few of the names are on the list of those I brought in. I don't know how it would be connected to Alida's parents. I think we have two separate cases, and we need to solve your case first. We need to go back to Alida's house and see what else you can get a read on. I really don't want you to come with me, but I'm not letting you out of my sight."

"It's our only hope."

When everyone was fed, bathed, and ready to go, Kirin and Talia held hands, then Alida grabbed both of them at the same time. There was a flash, and they landed in her home again. The trip was farther than the last one Alida had made. She'd gone pale, maybe because she had been using her gift so often.

Kirin picked her up her and swung her into his arms. Talia hunched over and waited for her head to stop spinning. The transport didn't seem to bother Kirin.

"Rest," Talia urged.

Kirin set Alida down on the couch and put a

blanket over her. Talia looked around the room. It looked like someone had been there. The furniture was turned over, almost like a fight had taken place.

"When I came to get Alida's items, I ran into a mercenary. He won't be a problem. His alpha told me he would make sure of it. If he tries to come after us again, I will burn his pack to the ground."

"That is a little extreme."

Kirin shrugged. "I will do anything to protect you and Alida."

Talia thought Kirin was being a little over the top, but she didn't have time to deal with his über-alpha side. She turned her attention to Alida. "Kirin will stay with you while I check out the kitchen."

Alida wrapped her arms around her body and sank farther into the couch. Kirin followed Talia into the kitchen.

"I need you to stay with Alida," Talia reminded him.

"What if someone shows up?"

"Then we should all be together."

"I'll go get her." Kirin started to turn.

"I don't want her in here. Her parents were killed here probably thirty-six hours ago. Think." She threw her hands in the air.

Kirin nodded and exited the room. Talia could

hear him talking to Alida. With both out of the room, she could concentrate on what she needed to do. It didn't matter how long an object sat before she touched it. A few years before, she'd touched a scepter that had belonged to King Tut. She had a vision of 1342 BC. King Tut gave orders to his men to go on a voyage. His palace was the most incredible thing she had ever seen. Gold lined the walls and ceiling. He wanted to rule the world. The anger and power she felt coming off of King Tut had put her in bed for three days. She didn't know how someone so young could have so much anger at the world. When she felt better, Talia researched the king and found out someone had assassinated him. Her vision made sense. He had sent his men out to figure out who was after his kingdom. No matter how cool it was to see the past, she didn't like experiencing the bad visions, and the one of King Tut was at the top of her bad-vision list.

Kirin helped settle her emotions but also silenced her gift. *What kind of crazy voodoo magic is that?* She moved to the blood spot she had touched the day before. There was something more for her to see. She just had to let the vision play out.

She laid her hand on it. Again, it started nicely. Maya was making dinner. Jalil had answered the door. Jalil and someone walked into the room, but the person was invisible to Talia. Jalil spoke to him. Maya even greeted the new guest. The person did nothing to hide his voice, but Talia didn't recognize it. He sat down at the kitchen chair. An argument started between Jalil and the mystery person. The report Jalil was working on needed to be altered, but Jalil refused. Then the guy told him that he knew he'd altered reports before. He said something about Alida. The way he said the name gave Talia chills. Jalil stood up and told him to leave. The man refused. He clicked something in his hand and raised his arms. Jalil's hands went to his throat. Maya let out a blood-curdling scream. Talia felt the scream all the way to her bones.

Maya grabbed the knife off the counter. Neither Maya nor Jalil could use their powers. Talia could feel not only the anguish in Maya but also the panic of not knowing why her powers didn't work. Maya ran toward the invisible image with the knife in her hands. She stopped a few steps away and grabbed her neck the way Jalil had. The intruder snapped both parents' necks and dropped them to the ground. Using the knife from Maya's hand, the intruder used his magic to stab both parents, never touching the blade. The blade clattered to the floor, and he stepped out of the room.

The anguish Maya felt for her daughter was thick in the room even after she passed. Talia could feel it deep down. Alida's mother had passed, only wanting her daughter to be protected. Talia reached up, wiped the tears from her face, and vowed to find Alida's mother's killer.

14
___

KIRIN

Kirin paced in the living room. Alida had fallen asleep. The magic she'd used to transport them had taken a lot out of her, and she would need to do it again soon. A picture on the wall caught his attention. Alida was with her parents, smiling, but what caught his eye was the farm in the background. It seemed familiar. Kirin felt as if he had seen the location before.

He walked over to the wall and grabbed the photo. Kirin flipped the picture over and took the photo out. It had no writing on the back. He slid the five-by-three-inch photo into his back pocket. Needing something to do, he studied the artwork on the wall. Alida must have drawn the pictures. Each one was of all three of them. The young girl was doing well for losing her parents. When they cleared her name, they would need to schedule an appointment with a therapist. Even though what had happened to her family was tragic, he couldn't help but smile at his makeshift family he was creating.

His eyes went from the hand-drawn picture of the family in front of a Christmas tree and landed on another photo, an image of the three of them in front of a waterfall, Alida holding a dog in her arms. Kirin walked back to the couch and sat next to Alida. He slowly shook her shoulder until she woke up.

She rubbed her eyes before turning in his direction. "Is it time to go?"

Kirin squeezed her shoulder. "Not yet, but I had a quick question." He held up the drawing from the wall. "Where is your puppy?"

Alida's lip quivered. "A wild animal got her one night when Dad let her go potty." She reached for the drawing in his hand and traced the dog.

"I'm sorry you lost your puppy. How long ago did this happen?"

"The day before my parents died."

Kirin's back went rigid at the information. The death of her dog had to be part of her parents' murder. Maybe whoever wanted them dead had taken care of the dog the day before, not wanting to risk the chance that the dog would alert the couple. Kirin couldn't hold back his anger. His dragon wanted to come forward and burn everything in sight. *How dare someone kill the young girl's doggy?*

"Thank you, precious. You can go back to sleep. We will wake you when we need to leave."

Alida bit her lip.

"What's on your mind?"

Tears filled her eyes. "Will I ever get to come back again and take my things and pictures of my parents?"

Kirin's old heart broke at her words. "Yes. When the case against you and Talia ends, I will help you pack whatever you want." He would destroy anyone who tried to stop him.

Something flickered out the window. Kirin rose from the couch and pulled back the curtain a little farther so he could view the front yard. Glancing around, he saw nothing. But to make sure, he walked back to the front door and flipped the dead bolt.

Talia had been in the kitchen long enough. When he peeked in, the need to protect her was at the forefront of his mind. Kirin could sense her anguish each time Talia touched the blood, and sadness wafted over him. Not only could he feel her sadness, but her need for sleep from using magic was strong as well. Talia and Alida were using their powers more than normal. They were getting little restful sleep. And their food was less than adequate. His dragon wanted to kill whoever had made Talia this sad.

And he knew, intrinsically, this is what having a mate meant: putting her needs before his and worrying over every little thing because her life impacted his. Once they finally mated, he'd be even more protective. Kirin was ready, but he had to make sure she was too.

Talia was sitting on the floor, tears streaming down her face as she touched the various blood spots. He understood why. She was touching Maya's blood. She was trying to find a way to vindicate Alida... and save them both.

He moved to her side. "You can do this, Talia. I believe in you," he whispered.

She sniffled and looked at him with watery eyes and a red face. "Thank you." She shook her head. "I can't see who. It's so strange. I can hear the man's voice, but I can't make out what he looks like from any angle. He used magic to kill then picked the knife up with magic. I'm sure Alida didn't kill her parents, but that will not be enough for Gideon... I think he wants her gone, but I don't understand why."

Kirin tilted his head. "Her powers. She hasn't even shown us the tip of the iceberg. I can feel them grow, and I think she is trying to hold back."

Talia licked her lips and stared at the spot of Maya's blood. "The only thing she worried about until her last breath was her daughter, but if he was after Alida, why didn't he take her?"

Kirin walked over and wrapped his arms around her waist. "Once they found her parents dead, there would be a search for the girl."

"So Gideon is after her, but the man in the vision didn't sound like Gideon."

"That doesn't mean Gideon doesn't have people working for him."

TALIA STEPPED out of Kirin arms and washed her hands in the sink. She could see that Maya's blood was off her hands but still felt it on her skin. Her emotions crawled through her mind. Days would pass before she no longer felt Maya's blood. And that was why she relied on her gloves so much.

"I'm not sure how to fix this." She shook her head.

"We will figure out who killed her parents."

His faith in her helped bolster her confidence and wipe away her sorrow. Standing up straighter, she murmured, "The laptop." She rushed from the kitchen and went straight to the office. Kirin moved like a true predator—she couldn't hear his footsteps behind her, but she could feel his presence.

He entered the office a few steps behind her. "What made you think to check the laptop?"

"A report. Jalil wouldn't change something in some report, and the killer was upset with him about that. That's what started all this. I don't think he planned to kill Jalil and Maya." She found the laptop and opened the lid.

"Someone killed Alida's dog the night before. I'm sure whoever this is that planned this attack knew Jalil wouldn't change the report. Do you know the password?" Kirin asked.

"Oh, my. They killed her puppy? We need to kill whoever hurt this family. I normally think they need a fair trial, but the man from my vision doesn't deserve that. As for the password, I figured out what Jalil used when I looked at the computer yesterday. But that time, I didn't know what I was looking for."

She scanned his recent documents. Then she decided to print them out—all of them. The printer was spitting out the papers, and Kirin was stuffing them in a folder he'd found in the cabinet.

As the last of the papers began to print out, he stiffened. "Did you hear that?"

Talia froze. She heard nothing, then there was the sound of a vehicle pulling up the driveway. She nodded. "We have to go."

He grabbed her, and they rushed to Alida on the couch. The little girl's eyes were wide open. She knew what was happening or sensed that something was off. She held out her hands to them, and as soon as they touched, there was a flash, and they landed back in Talia's grandparents' cabin. There was no fire going—they'd smothered it before they left. And now they were trying to decide whether or not to start one again.

"Let's wrap you in a sleeping bag," Talia suggested as she pulled one out of the closet. "These sleeping bags are made for thirty below. We'll make food, and you warm up and rest." The little girl didn't fight the sleep. She passed out on the couch within minutes.

Talia and Kirin walked over to the table and sat down with the stack of papers she'd printed out. When her bare hand touched him, she thought an onset of images would hound her. But they didn't. She grabbed his hand again. Nothing. *How can this be?*

Needing to know if her powers had disappeared, she reached for a knife on the table. A vision of her grandmother and grandfather eating dinner came alive. Grandpa Joe joked about the meatloaf Grandma had cooked. Talia kept the vision going a couple more seconds. She missed her grandparents, but she also felt like she was intruding into a private memory. She dropped the knife, and the vision vanished.

Talia looked at Kirin. "I need to talk to you alone."

He nodded. "Whatever you need, Talia." He followed her down the hall to her grandparents' room.

As soon as they entered the room, she shut the door behind him. "I don't understand what's happening between us. I don't even understand what you are."

"I'm a dragon shifter," he murmured.

Talia rolled her eyes. "Of course you are a dragon shifter, but what does that mean, and why the hell can't I stay away from you? Why do I long for your touch? Why do I feel like I'm missing a piece of myself if you're not near?"

He licked his lips. "Because we're meant to be mated."

"What do you mean, *mated*?"

Kirin sat down on the bed and pulled her into his lap. "What do you know about shifters?"

Her body melted into his. "You can shift." His deep chuckle made her body come alive. "Not much else, besides that you heal fast."

He slowly ran his hand along her back. "Hmm... there is only one person made for me." Kirin leaned forward and planted a kiss on her shoulder.

"How can you be so sure?" Talia wished she had done research on shifters.

"My dragon picked you."

"Just like that, your dragon declares we are together until we die?" She could feel Kirin smile as his lips touched her shoulder before he nipped the skin.

"Sort of."

Talia pulled back. "Sort of *what*? When your dragon gets tired, you ditch me?"

"No. Once we mate, you will become immortal like me." Kirin put his lips to her mouth. "That doesn't mean we can't die, but it's hard as fuck to kill us. We will be together forever. Do you have any other questions?"

"Yes—two. Will I turn into a dragon when you bite me? And do you have a hoard like dragons in the movies have?"

Kirin huffed. "There is nothing wrong with having a hoard. And no—you will not turn into a dragon. You will stay human but live forever. Our children will be dragons and might have your abilities."

Talia had never thought about children. She worried what would happen if she ever married a human and her children had powers. With Kirin, so many possibilities opened for the future. But before she would commit to mating, she needed to know if he could walk away if he didn't want her anymore.

"I want to keep Alida."

"Of course we are keeping her. Anyone who tries to stand in our way will die."

She didn't completely understand the whole

mating thing, but she wanted to. "Show me," she urged.

"We can't go back once we mate," he told her.

" I have this strong feeling we need to mate. I don't know if it's from what is happening around us or what. But I don't care. Mating feels right." She nodded. "I'll take my chances. I need this."

"Show me. I'm here. I want to be your mate."
She slid her arms around his waist. Kirin's dragon let out a rumble.

Kirin rested his two-day-whiskered chin on top of her head and slid his arms around her. Talia relaxed into his arms. She didn't know how much more she could want him. Being next to him felt like everything in her life had fallen into place. It felt like the first breath of fresh air after a wave in the ocean took her for a tumble.

Over the past day, she'd felt as if the ocean current had sucked her to the bottom of the ocean floor and she had no clue if she would see the light of day. And then Kirin had appeared in the cabin. No matter how hard she tried, he had an effect on her.

Talia never imagined finding someone to spend the rest of her life with. Her inability to touch anyone without gloves made dating hard... but as she stood in her grandparents' bedroom, touching Kirin with her bare hands, all that mattered was that they made sense together.

"You are the most beautiful woman I've ever seen," he whispered. His voice held need. "I want to take this slow, but my dragon is pushing to claim you."

"I don't want you to hold back."

His chest rumbled at her words. A minute passed before he murmured, "You deserve to be treated like a princess."

She leaned back so she could see his eyes. His dragon was so close to the surface that Kirin's eyes glowed gold in the dark room.

"I never thought I would end up with anyone," she said, licking her lips. "You came chasing after Alida and me, and now I don't know if I could ever run from you."

"I will protect you and the little girl in the living room with all my strength."

Her eyes never left his. "I know. I didn't need to read your mind to know how much you care about both of us. But what will happen if you can't keep me out of jail? Maybe you shouldn't tie yourself to me until we know I'm in the clear."

"Mmm," he murmured, running his hands down her back. "No one will take you from me. I will work until my last breath, making sure we clear your name. If we can't figure out how, I will take you and Alida into hiding."

Talia huffed. "We aren't going into hiding. I have faith we will figure out what Gideon is doing and clear our names."

The corners of his beautiful lips turned up. "Strong mate."

Talia couldn't hold back any longer. She pushed up on her tiptoes and pressed her lips to his. Kirin brushed her lips with his. She didn't know how such a dangerous man could be so gentle against her lips. Her body yearned for a taste. He swiped his tongue across her lips. She opened immediately, needing more of him. The world was crashing down around them, but all was right at that moment. *Is this love?* Time passed around them—she didn't know how long they spent kissing. But she didn't want to pull back. Kirin ran his hands down her back and grabbed her ass. Her body melted farther into his hard, tough body.

Kirin gripped her backside and lifted her up.

Talia immediately wrapped her legs around him. His lips felt soft as he kissed her. Kirin slowly lowered her to the bed, and when he pulled back, his eyes were bright. He leaned back down and pressed his luscious lips to hers, and his weight on her felt good, like one of those weighted blankets that make people feel protected and safe. She had her own human one that she never planned to let go of. His lips left hers and trailed down her jaw, stopping at her ear to suck. Talia couldn't hold back the moan. She ran her nails down his back, wanting to leave her mark, her claim. Kirin followed the line from her ear to her neck and bit down slightly before pulling back. Her body hummed with need.

He trailed kisses down her neck to the edge of her T-shirt. Kirin's fingers pulled at the edge of her shirt and helped her pull it over her head. He let out a groan as she lay back down in her white lace bra.

"Beautiful," he mumbled between kisses on her collarbone. His eyes flashed between bright gold and brown when he looked up between kisses, and seeing the man and beast want her sparked her need. As if knowing what she thought, he gave her a cocky smile.

Down, down—Kirin continued his journey down her body. She gasped as he ran his tongue above the top of her jeans. Her hips rolled up, demanding his trip downward. "Do you want something, my mate?"

"Please, Kirin, I need you."

She felt Kirin slowly unbuckle her jeans and pull them down her legs. He leaned down and kissed her thigh and inner leg as he worked his way down. When he made his way up, he stopped at her inner leg and placed butterfly kisses. She sucked in her breath. She'd never had a man put his mouth on her that way. Her insecurities about not being very experienced crept to the surface. As he licked over her slit, those feelings were replaced with a dire need. Her body felt like it was on fire. She needed more and less at the same time. She trembled with each touch and lick from Kirin.

"I want to feel you in me."

"Not yet," he purred, and he swiped his tongue deep inside her.

She couldn't hold back the moan as she worked her hands into his silky black hair, and with each stroke of his tongue, she was further lost in the ecstasy. He slid his arms around her legs, pulling her hips up. His head bobbed between her legs as he went between, licking and kissing. She didn't know if he would ever stop or how much longer she could take hanging on edge. Her nub was sensitive, and she didn't know how much longer she could hold on before falling.

The rumbling of Kirin's dragon between her legs vibrated her whole body when she went over the edge to climax. His dragon rumbled harder, and he pushed his tongue into her. Her body felt as if it floated between the licking, the rumbling, and his magic fingers.

Kirin licked one more time before sitting up and ripping his shirt off. Talia trained her eyes on his perfectly sculpted body. His abs flexed as he worked to unfastened his jeans in a hurry. He crawled back up her body, slowly kissing along the way. The fire in her body burned for him when his hard dick was near. She pressed her hips, trying to get closer to him. Kirin fed her need and buried himself deep. His movement was hard and fast, his powerful body tensing as he slammed into her. She lifted her hips with each thrust and met him each time. He gripped her hair and held her head so his eyes could focus on her. It was so intense she almost came under his control. She closed her eyes to hold on to the ecstasy for a few moments longer.

"I want to see your eyes," Kirin growled.

His hard cock throbbed inside her. She couldn't hold back any longer. Her body pulsed around his.

As they both went over the edge, Kirin lowered his head and bit her shoulder. She thought it would hurt when his teeth went into her flesh, but it was the opposite—her body continued to ride the wave as Kirin pumped into her. She screamed out his name in pure ecstasy.

"Mmm, my mate," he whispered as he licked his bite mark. "Do you feel okay? Did I hurt you?"

"No, it doesn't hurt. Tingles a little."

"You are the most amazing woman—strong, protective, and beautiful." Kirin's lips turned up. "You will make the rest of eternity interesting."

Talia couldn't hold back her smile as she lay in Kirin's arms. She wondered if every time would feel like this. She wasn't sure she ever wanted to leave the bed. Kirin's member rubbed against her leg, and she felt him get hard again.

"How?"

Kirin's chuckle rumbled through her body. "You, my mate."

Talia grabbed his member in her hand and enjoyed the rumble from Kirin's dragon. This time around, she planned to give him pleasure.

16
KIRIN

With Talia around, he'd forgotten everything but her. Mostly, he'd forgotten Conley's birthday. Kia would be all up his butt over that. Conley's birthday was an excuse to make the three of them spend time together. Kirin knew the call would come that day, but he bet it would be from his mother. Over the past few years, they had spent less and less time together. Kirin had slowly distanced himself from his brothers.

He stared down at Talia in his arms. Even without the fire going, they were plenty warm. Being near her started the fire inside him. He would be all the more dangerous now. He'd never be able to let anything happen to her. They were mated.

She stirred in his arms and stared up at him. "Will it always be like that?"

He ran his knuckles down her cheek. "That was me claiming you."

She nodded. "I'm worn out but invigorated at the same time. Explain." She was so serious, so determined. He loved this about her.

"I've heard that the claiming has side effects for the new mate." He licked his lips and bent to kiss her. "As we talked about earlier, you will be immortal as long as I live."

Her brow furrowed. "Is there anything else besides immortality?"

"I've never looked into mating much or what happens when you find a mate." Kirin murmured. "You're already supernatural. We'll have to figure out the rest of the changes as we go."

"How could you not know about mating?"

Kirin leaned over and kissed the tip of Talia's nose. "Honestly, I never thought I would find my mate. I've been alive over three hundred years." When Talia pulled back, he said, "Don't take that the wrong way. I'm happy I found you. When we clear your name, we will figure everything out. We have the rest of our lives."

Talia bit her lip.

"Ask your question, Talia. Don't ever be afraid to ask me anything."

She let out a breath and rushed her words. "Will we be able to have kids?"

Kirin didn't have time to answer. His phone rang on the end table. Maybe they weren't as far out in the middle of nowhere as he believed. He glanced at the screen. "Kia." He sighed. "I'm in trouble. Give me a minute."

He could feel her watching as he left the bed, dressed, and answered the call. "Kia." He waited.

"You forgot. I knew you'd forget. What's your excuse this time?"

Kirin felt slight sadness for letting his brother down, but his priority was to protect Alida and Talia. Once he explained, Kia would understand. Kirin ran his hand through his hair. "I didn't forget or miss coming to your house on purpose."

Kia huffed on the other end. "Mom is cursing your name. You've been slowly distancing yourself from Conley and me for years. Why?"

Kirin didn't know why, but over the years, his dragon wanted more and more solitude. He grumbled when they had to work. Kirin let his dragon have his way. He still felt responsible for his dad's death. He knew there was nothing he could have done to protect them. He'd avenged his death, but when he looked at his younger siblings, he felt guilty for the fact that they didn't have their dad around.

Needing a couple more seconds before answering Kia, Kirin slipped on his shirt, but as he did, he heard activity outside. His eyes widened. *Time's up.*

"They found us," he hissed at Talia. She jumped off the bed and grabbed her clothes from the night before.

"Who found you?" Kia asked.

Kirin didn't have time to explain to his brother what was about to go down. He would tell him everything in a few minutes. "Where are you?" Kirin asked Kia.

Kia responded immediately. "My house."

Talia had finished putting her clothes on. They raced to the living room. The fire was out, and Alida was curled up on the couch in her sleeping bag. Kirin could hear the sound of boots crushing the snow. Three separate men were outside the house. He let his dragon come out a little to see if he could sense who the intruders were. If he didn't have to worry about Talia and Alida, he would let his dragon out for an afternoon snack.

Kirin's dragon growled when he sensed a wolf

outside. It seemed he would have to eat a whole pack once this was over. He rushed toward Alida and lifted her then looked back to see why Talia wasn't by his side. She was at the kitchen table, grabbing the papers they'd needed to look over the night before.

With Alida in his arms, he took a couple of steps across the cabin to Talia's side. Once she was within arm's reach, he said, "The place in my head," and closed his eyes to think. "Got it?"

She nodded. They were gripping each other when the front door exploded open, and they left the cabin in a flash of light. He wasn't able to get a look at the intruders. When he opened his eyes, they had all landed in a pile in his brother's living room.

"What the fuck?" Kia screamed. He still had his phone to his ear—he hadn't hung up on their conversation.

Conley came racing into the room. Kirin glanced at the clock. "I'm only a day late, little brother."

Their bodies were tangled on the floor. Luckily, Talia and Alida lay on top of him. Talia slowly stood up, and Alida climbed to the side. Kirin stood up and dusted off the broken coffee table they'd landed on.

"You didn't miss the coffee table either." Conley

snickered.

Kia shook his head. "You're going to replace that."

"How was I supposed to know you moved the coffee table to that location? The table wasn't there last time I was here. Of course, I will buy you a new table. Send me the bill," Kirin said.

"Sorry. I didn't get the memo that we are supposed to tell you when we move furniture. You will buy all matching furniture. I highly doubt I can find a matching set."

Kirin's brow arched. "Don't push it. What do you need a matching set for? The coffee table didn't match anything, and you can afford new furniture." He glanced around. Kia had lived in the same house for the last two hundred years, a small two-bedroom cabin on the side of the mountain. The only item on the white walls was a seventy-inch TV. He also had an old brown couch. "You could afford a whole new place."

Kia glared at him.

But if Kirin had to bet, Kia's office would be decked out with the latest technology. Kia had his family pictures up in his office, where he spent most of his time.

"Why do I need a better place?" Kia smirked.

"Good luck attracting a mate here."

Kirin's mom chose that moment to walk into the living room. "What do you know about having a mate, dear?" She walked over and kissed him on the cheek. "I've been after you for years, and you've ignored my request for grandkids."

Kirin looked in Talia's direction. Then Kia stared at Talia. She bit her lower lip and looked to Kirin for direction.

"No fucking way," Kia said. "I thought you were joking."

Kirin's mom turned her eyes on her middle child. "You knew he found his mate and didn't tell me?"

Kia pointed at Kirin. "He told me not to." For being over two hundred years old, he still acted like a two year old.

Kirin held up his hands for everyone to be quiet. "This is Talia. My mate."

"And she has a kid?" his mother asked.

"This is Alida." Talia took a deep breath. "And we are outlaws."

Kirin pulled her into his arms. He could feel the pain, and he suffered with her. He liked that her powers weren't as affected now when they touched. He couldn't imagine not being able to touch her all the time.

Kia leveled a look at Kirin, waiting.

"Gideon," Kirin muttered by way of explanation. "You were right, Kia. He is up to something. We need to figure out what."

Talia turned to smile at Conley. "Happy belated birthday. What are you... twenty-five?" She grinned.

"Two hundred thirty-four," he replied proudly.

Her jaw dropped, and everyone laughed. "But you're the youngest." Talia turned her blue eyes on Kirin. "How old are you?"

Alida giggled. "Kirin is three hundred fifty-four."

"Wow," Talia mumbled. "You are immortal."

Kirin pulled her into his arms. "Are you saying I'm too old for you?"

"What? No, it just made the immortal thing click a little more hearing how old you are."

Conley chuckled. "Even your mate thinks you're old."

"Let's have some cake, and we can talk about the outlaws we are hiding," Judy, Kirin's mom, suggested.

Alida piped up. "I like cake."

"Give the kid some cake." Kirin laughed. "And then... talk."

He gave Talia a look. He hoped she could read him. In case she couldn't, he held out his hand. Taking a deep breath, she reached out to grasp it with both hands. Kirin reached out his other hand and grasped Alida's little hand. The young girl looked up with a smile on her lips. It melted his heart. His life had seemed so boring until he met these two.

Kirin had forgotten how much he like being around his brothers. He missed the easy banter. Everyone was around Kia's dining room table, eating chocolate cake. Kirin knew he needed to start spending more time with his brothers. Over the years he had let his work life rule his real life. It was time to change.

Conley focused his red eyes on him. "So, what is going on? Why are you two on the run?"

"This can wait until we are done with cake."

Conley waved his fork. "No. I want to hear what is going on and what we need to do to protect you."

Kirin had always known his brothers would have his back. They spent the next half hour talking about Alida and why they thought Gideon was part of this.

"Well, fuck," Conley said.

"That's a bad word," Alida said with a full mouth of cake.

Everyone around the table chuckled. "Yes, it is, and I promise not to say it out loud," Talia said.

Kirin turns toward Alida, "Don't read their minds either."

At that, Kia spat his swig of beer across the table. He looked at the young girl. "You can read my mind?"

Alida shrugged. "You're kind of boring to read. Too much stuff about computers and someone named Antheia." She turned her eyes on his youngest brother. "You swear a lot. If we had a swear jar, I would be rich." When Alida turned toward his mom, Judy held a finger to her lips. Alida giggled. "Your secrets are safe with me."

Everyone around the table laughed except Conley, who complained about not being warned about the young girl's ability to read minds.

Kirin looked at each of his brothers. "Nobody can find out about her powers. The most they know is she can transport. But her parents had her on medication for the past few years. I'm not sure even if they knew the extent of her powers. Each day I'm with her, I can feel them grow. That's why we think Gideon is after her."

Conley twisted his beer in his hands. "I will do everything I can to protect her. She is part of us now."

Kirin knew what the words meant. Conley's

dragon had accepted her and would do anything in his power to protect her.

Kia looked at the young girl with admiration. "We'll do everything we can to protect her."

Alida giggled. "Your dragon is loud and funny. I'm trying not to listen, but he keeps saying I'm his to protect. He keeps grumbling about digital killing anyone who wants to hurt me."

Kia shrugged. "My dragon likes technology, and he likes you."

"Why don't you take Talia and Alida and go on the run, Kia," Kirin said, "and I'll stay back and figure out how to deal with Gideon." Kirin's dragon had been on edge, not liking that someone was after the two people he had grown to care about.

"No!" Talia shouted. All eyes turned in her direction. "Alida and I are not going into hiding. We will figure out who is after us together."

Alida dropped her fork onto the plate, and the sound echoed through the room. "I don't want to leave your side, Talia." Tears formed in the young girl's eyes. That was one sight his dragon didn't like to see.

"How about we take one hour at a time? At this moment, Talia and I aren't going to leave you."

17

TALIA

W*ell, this is one way to meet the family.* Talia had lost her family years before, and now she had two brothers-in-law, a child, and a mother-in-law. Her life had been calm, even bordering on boring, but she hadn't been running from the council. And now her life was in shambles. She joked about being an outlaw, but as someone who had used her gift for nothing her entire life but taking down criminals, this was a huge change, and she struggled with it.

What am I supposed to do with my life now? How am I going to stay out of jail or even alive? Will Alida and I be on the run the rest of our lives? Can I keep this up? One look at the young girl answered her questions. She would run forever to protect Alida.

Kia and Conley gathered the dishes from the table. Alida yawned beside her. The amount of energy needed to transport the three of them to Kia's house had drained her again. They needed to stop using the young girl's gift.

"She can lie down in Kia's room while we figure out what we are going to do."

"I don't want to go to bed again," Alida complained while she rubbed her eyes.

Talia reached over and tucked a wayward hair behind Alida's ear. "We need you to have energy. Kirin and I are going to do everything we can to protect you, but we need to come up with a plan so you don't have to keep using your powers."

Alida yawned again. "Okay."

Judy stood from the table. "Let me take her into the living room."

Talia hesitated, not wanting to drop Alida's hand.

"I'll be fine, Talia. Judy is good." Alida let go of Talia's hand and reached for Judy's. Talia watched as they left the dining room.

"I do trust y—"

Kirin held up a finger to her mouth. "You don't have to explain."

He grabbed Talia's hand. Not only did his touch soothe her like some kind of dragon-shifter-shaped

Xanax, but she could also touch him without memories flooding her. It seemed he could now control what she could see.

Talia's breath hitched when she watched the vision Kirin pushed at her. This time, it wasn't a memory. It was the future. She could tell because of her sizeable bump. And they weren't alone. They were at a playground—the same one Talia had played at when she was a young girl. Her mom and dad would take her there every Sunday for a few hours. Some of her greatest memories with her parents were of time spent at that park. Talia's eyes started to tear up as she watched Alida run around, playing with other kids. She was happy, they were happy, and most of all, they were all alive and free.

"Is this real?" she asked, feeling hopeful for the first time.

He nodded. Kirin tugged at her arm, causing her to fly into his embrace. He pressed his lips to hers and pulled back. "This is what I see when I look at you. When you asked the question earlier if we could have kids, this image floated through my mind. I knew we would be able to. It looks like our children will have both of our gifts. It's strange—I get snippets of the life we'll have. This... seems to be my new gift."

Her brow furrowed. "Is this a thing? You get some of me, and I get some of you?"

Kirin tightened his arms around her. "It's new for us."

Conley pulled out the chair at the dining room table with another beer in hand. Kia followed suit and sat down next to them. "Have you looked at the reports you printed off Jalil's computer?" Kia asked.

Kirin pulled out the folder from his back pocket and set it on the table. "We meant to look at it last night, but something came up."

Conley snickered, and Talia blushed a deep red. Kirin reached over and squeezed her hand.

"Also the warlock that showed up gave us a file. The file contained a list of missing or killed council leaders. Some of the people on the list I brought in. But I don't think their reports are tied to this report."

Kia set his bottle down. "Let me see what the warlock gave you."

Kirin slid the folder across the table.

Talia was paging through the papers they had printed out. "These seem to be closed cases. But is this one"—Talia pointed to the report—"the warlock you brought in?"

Kirin glanced over. "Yes. And no, I don't recognize the name."

"So what did Gideon want changed? I never caught what he wanted Jalil to change."

"Fuck," Kia mumbled. "Remember I told you something wasn't right? Half of the people in these reports the warlocks gave you are ones I've looked into."

The four sat around the table for another hour before Kia cleared his throat. "Well, I guess it's time to let you in on my secret."

"You have a secret?" Conley's eyes widened.

"We don't keep secrets from each other, and normally, you can't keep a secret," Conley grumbled.

Kia shook his head. "I used to be like that. Then things changed around here. They are subtle changes. You wouldn't notice."

"Explain," Conley demanded.

Kirin frowned, and Talia imagined it was because he was the older brother and expected to know it all or at least be on top of everything. Talia had never had a sibling to share these types of things with. She glanced toward the living room, where Alida and Kirin's mom had gone. She couldn't wait to give the young girl a brother or sister. In less than two days, Talia had come to feel as if she was Alida's mom.

Kia launched into his explanation. "Carter and I

landed a large contract with a government contractor. We are building new labs for them, for environmental research to preserve the mountains. This means something to Carter and me. Both of us have put money into the company. But our laborers are going missing, and then they reappear a few days later with no explanation. Some people return after lengthy absences, and they are different... off. If I didn't know better, I'd think they were clones. I can't put my finger on it, but I have changed up the way I do business and the way I live. This... is my public house, the one everyone knows about, the place where I get my mail."

"Could be the builders," Kirin pointed out.

Kia laughed. "You'd think so, right?" Then he shook his head. "I had a vampire foreman on the site. He compelled everyone to forget."

Kirin frowned. "And what of him?"

Kia leaned in. "Let's just say he's aware of my abilities, and since fire is one of their immortality killers, he doesn't want to mess with me." He shrugged. "So, you coming or what?"

Talia crawled off Kirin's lap, and they walked to the living room, where Judy and Alida were talking.

"Hey, Mom and Alida, we are going to check out Kia's secret." They followed Kia as he led them into a garage with four state-of-the-art cars, one of which Talia didn't even recognize. Kirin must have noticed her staring. "Kia likes new technology. Most of the auto manufacturers let him demo cars."

Conley let out a chuckle. "Let's be serious. The money he invests into these companies is the reason he gets the latest car. If he could wait until they came out, he would save tons of money."

Kia placed his hand on the wall, and a silver car she'd had no clue existed rose ten feet in the air on a platform. Talia looked down at what looked like a marble floor. Kia walked over to the middle of the floor and placed his hand on it. A screen appeared, and he entered a password. A six-by-six-foot section of the floor opened, revealing two staircases.

"How?" Talia asked.

"The floor design is a mix of technology and state-of-the-art building materials."

Kia stood on the top stair. "Are you coming or not?" He continued downward.

Kirin tugged at her hand. When she didn't take a step, Alida turned to her. "It's okay, my future mommy. Kia's place is cool."

Talia's eyes watered at hearing Alida call her mom. She reached out and held the girl's hand. The three of them followed Kia down the stairs. Conley followed closely behind, grumbling, "Happy birthday to me. My brother's keeping secrets, and I don't have any tinfoil to keep the young girl out of our heads."

"You're silly, Uncle Conley. Tinfoil won't keep me out. You and Kia need to stop thinking so loud."

Conley reached forward and picked Alida up. "You are my new favorite girl."

Alida's laughter echoed through the stairwell as Conley tickled her sides. They went down a few more feet to the bottom of the stairs then entered a square room.

"The floor moving was more impressive than this." Conley pointed out.

The eight-by-eight-foot cement room reminded Talia of a cell. When she looked back up at the top of the stairs, the floor had closed.

Kia turned his back on Conley. "This is just another layer of security." He placed his hand on the wall again, and an elevator appeared.

The six stepped into the gold-plated elevator. Talia was still worried not knowing where they were going. Each of them was blindly following Kirin's brother to a place no one knew about.

"Do you keep your hoard in a secret lair also?" Talia asked Kirin as they went down the elevator.

She hated elevators. She needed a distraction from her fear of dropping to her death. Most elevators at least let people know how many floors they might drop. She couldn't find anything on the wall to let her know what floor they were on.

Kirin threw his head back and laughed. "I highly doubt Kia is taking us anywhere near his hoard." He glanced at his brothers and then back at her. "When this is over, I will take you to see my hoard." Kirin's brothers took in their breath and looked at him, alarmed. He said, "When you find your mate, you will understand."

"Antheia, prepare for guests," Kia said.

"Yes, sir. Do you want me to have coffee ready for them?"

Talia looked around the elevator to find out how the woman was responding to or seeing them.

"Really?" Conley mumbled.

"Yes, please," Kia said. "And hot chocolate."

The lift continued downward. Talia gripped Kirin's hands as the platform below moved. They had been on the elevator for five minutes before it started to slow down. When it stopped, Kia placed his hand on the gold wall, and a screen lit up. A device scanned Kia's face again before a secret panel in the wall opened.

When the door opened, Talia rushed out of the elevator. What she saw was the last thing she expected. She'd thought the door would open onto something like Batman's cave. It was the total opposite. Light shone through the floor-to-ceiling windows. The sun bounced off the crisp white marble floors. The view was breathtaking. Kia's cabin could have fit in the entryway of his secret hideout.

Kirin grinned. "Multiple escape points, I assume."

Kia laughed. "You're correct, sir."

On the coffee table in the center of the room sat three coffee cups and a mug of hot chocolate. The gold table had to cost more money than Talia had made in her whole lifetime. Talia looked around, trying to figure out where the woman had gone.

"Antheia is computer operated," Kia said. "She had the machine make the coffee, and I have a robot who delivered it to the table."

"Umm, I thought you invested in companies."

Kia let out a chuckle. "That is what I do. But I love to create machines."

Conley stood to the side with his arms crossed and a scowl on his face. "How long have you had this place?"

Kia pinched the bridge of his nose. "I built it four years ago."

Conley stormed out of the room toward the back of the lair. Talia chuckled to herself. Kia the dragon had a lair.

Kia made a move as if about to follow his younger brother, but Kirin reached out and gripped his shoulder. "Give him a second. You kept something huge from him. Conley just needs time to come to grips with all of this. You have to admit, this is a huge thing to keep from your brothers."

"I know. I plan to tell you everything going forward. Do you think he will forgive me?"

"Yes. Now, show us around." Kirin turned toward his mom. "You don't seem surprised."

"A mother always knows."

"I never said anything," Kia said.

Judy shrugged and walked toward the open room. Talia followed everyone through the main living area. She could see that there were multiple floors and stairs leading up and down. On the far wall were windows and sliding patio doors leading out to a balcony. As she drew near, she realized he'd built the house into the face of a cliff.

Talia gasped. "Wow."

18

KIRIN

Kirin stopped in front of the large window and gazed at the mountain valley. "I wished you'd told us you suspected something was wrong. We would have been here for you."

Kia scoffed. "I tried to tell you multiple times over the years that I didn't trust Gideon. You never seemed to care."

His younger brother was right. Kirin had cared more about the money and finishing cases. He hadn't spent much time figuring out if the person he was after was really up to no good. *How many people did I turn in or kill who didn't deserve it?*

"Gideon will send people to my house next. Hell,

they might already be there." Kirin heard Talia's breath hitch. "It's okay, Talia. I don't keep anything important in my main house. Kia isn't the only one with a secret lair."

"You're more than welcome to stay here with me until this is all settled," Kia said.

"You know, your security is impressive. And no one knows about this place?" Kirin shook his head. "Well, then, as long as we are not an imposition..."

"Kirin, I have almost ten thousand hidden square feet. Conley, you should probably stay too. And I'll tell the office I'm working from home for a bit." He shrugged. "The benefits of being the boss."

"Oh, goody. A sleepover for my birthday," Conley joked. Kirin could still hear the hurt in his voice.

"Gideon won't stop at sending people to your house. He'll send people to Conley's house, and even —" Talia's head whipped from side to side. "Where is she? Where did she go?" Pure panic laced her voice. She reached out, tears forming in her pure blue eyes. Kirin's gut turned with Talia's anguish. Before he had time to respond, though, Alida reappeared. Talia dropped to her knees in front of the girl and grabbed her hands. "What happened, Alida? Where did you go?"

Alida frowned. "I had to check. I can't use my abilities everywhere."

Talia pulled the young girl into her arms. "Don't ever disappear without letting me know first. You scared me." Talia squeezed Alida one more time before standing. "What do you mean you can't always use your abilities?"

"Like in the cars on the way to the council building. You know... the one that looks like a warehouse. And the warehouse, too, until that minute... the air changed, and I knew I could. That's why we left when we did." Alida smiled at them. She sank down into the living room chair. "I'm tired. And hungry. Can I have more cake?"

Shaking his head, Kirin murmured, "We need to make sure you have some healthy foods. We have to keep your strength up. We need you strong, not in a sugar coma. Got it?"

She giggled. "It was worth a try."

Kirin turned in his brother's direction. "Well, you heard the girl. She's hungry. Does your secret lair have food?"

Kia walked toward the kitchen. "What does everyone want? We have steak, chicken, or seafood."

"Steak," everyone said in unison.

Kia took a few steaks and put them on the grill

out on the deck. Conley grabbed everyone a beer, and the group sat out there. Kia had enclosed the area, and the temperature was the same as in the house.

Conley pointed his beer in Kirin and Talia's direction. "Is that what being mated is like?" His voice was full of longing.

"What do you mean?" Kia asked. "Kirin has acted the same as he always does."

"No, look at them. It's like they've been together forever." Conley shook his head in wonder.

Kia mumbled, "I could use a mate—someone to keep me grounded, rock my world, that kind of thing." He sighed.

Alida wasn't the only hungry one. Everyone around the table ate quietly, lost in thought. When the girl placed her fork and knife down, her eyes kept trying to close.

"You ready for bed, princess?" Talia asked.

"No, I want to stay up with everyone else." She couldn't even keep her eyes open while she talked.

Talia stood from the chair on the balcony. "Come on, Alida. Let's go find you a bedroom."

"She can take a room down the left hall. There is another room that connects to it."

Kirin thanked his brother for creating an

amazing hiding home and followed Talia and Alida down the hall. The young girl's feet dragged as she walked down the hallway. Her room on the left was light blue. The windows overlooked the mountain range. Each room in Kia's house impressed Kirin.

Alida crawled up onto the bed. "Can I have a good-night hug?"

Talia rushed to her side, hugged the young girl, and placed a kiss on her forehead. Alida giggled at something Talia whispered in her ear. When Talia pulled back, the little girl's eyes swung to Kirin. There was no way he couldn't give the girl a good-night hug. He wrapped his muscled arms around the girl. She was so young and fragile. His dragon promised to protect her.

"Good night, princess."

"Good night, Kirin."

Kirin pulled Talia out of the room and shut the light off. Talia let out a startled squeak. His mom was standing outside the door.

"I'm going to sleep in the other bedroom next to hers," Judy said. "Don't worry about her tonight. I remember what it was like when your father and I first mated. Enjoy the night."

Talia stared at the closed door.

"She will be safe," Judy said.

"I know. She scared me earlier when she disappeared." Talia closed her eyes and sighed. "Thank you, Judy. Good night."

Kirin leaned over and kissed his mom's forehead. Talia gave her a hug before they headed down to their room.

"Kirin, I know I've only known her for a couple of days, but she's wiggled into my heart. It's crazy how much I want to protect her."

Kirin wrapped his arms around Talia. "Those are your feelings. Nothing is wrong with them. I know how you feel. My dragon wants to go burn the whole council down. He doesn't even care if not everyone in the council worked with Gideon. He wants Gideon to pay."

"Do you think we will ever be safe?"

"I will do everything in my power to make sure you and Alida are safe. Now, let's have another beer with my brothers before bed."

It was well after midnight when Kirin sat down with his brothers. Kia had started a fire out on the deck.

"Do you think they will find us with the fire?" Talia asked Kia.

"Nope. I've had the valley of the mountain enchanted by three different witches. The only thing anyone will ever see is a mountain surface. The witches also protect this area so nobody can come around here. And I've had state-of-the-art sensors put in, so we'll know far in advance if anyone is near."

Conley picked at the beer label. "I don't understand how the intruder overpowered Maya and Jalil."

Talia ran her hand through her hair. "This should've clicked earlier when Alida didn't know if she could transport. The council has something to block powers. I thought it was strange when I heard a click in the vision and none of their powers worked. Whoever came into the house had to have used it on her parents. The man who killed them must've done something to make him immune. And the council must have turned the device off when I went into the room. I couldn't have used my powers if it was on. That was when Alida could use her powers again."

Kia leaned back in his chair. "We know Gideon wants the girl. Why risk you touching the knife?"

"Gideon knew I wouldn't be able to see anything and he could still keep up his front with the rest of the council. Kael pushed for me to come in."

Kia stared at Talia. "We need to figure out if it's a

device or spell. How many people in the council are corrupt like Gideon?" Kia tapped his bottle on the table. "I bet they used a device to cut Alida's and her parents' abilities. But messing with your vision has to be a spell. So we know he has Carter's pack working with him and a witch."

Talia leaned forward. "Don't forget the dark man. Also, we don't know it's the whole pack. Jeremiah is corrupt, and we haven't talked to Carter again."

"What else can you tell us about the vision?" Conley asked.

"My vision was... altered. Someone had messed with it. They wiped the dark man out. Someone had cleaned the vision up, edited, to make it look like Alida killed her parents. What could do that?" She frowned.

The guys shook their heads. "I could ask around," Kia mumbled. "There's a lab I plan to check into. We have a partnership with them. Maybe this will turn up something."

"Maybe." Talia curled up in Kirin's arms. He held her close.

Kirin looked off into the skyline. They kept going in circles with no answers. He reached for the report. "This name sounds so familiar, but I can't figure out why. The report was an investigation into a warlock for using dark magic. The council forbids dark magic and could put you in prison for using it. Jalil's report stated the warlock didn't use dark magic."

"I remember in the vision Jalil argued with the intruder over the report. The man who killed Alida's parents wanted her dad to change the report. Alida's dad refused to do that."

Kia reached over and grabbed the report. "Fuck." He paged to the end. "This is the warlock Gideon killed."

Kirin's blood boiled. "No, it's not. His name was Zyra."

Kia leveled a look at him. "They gave you a different name. You brought this man."

"So he wanted the report changed so he could cover the fact he had an innocent man killed."

Kirin leaned back in his chair. "I wish we could project part of your vision. I think it would be enough to clear Alida. The vision would show another person there. Once we cleared your names, we could figure out why Gideon wanted this warlock dead. I don't understand why he would go after a council member from another state."

Talia jumped from her seat and ran to grab her phone. "I don't know why I didn't think of this earlier. I have a friend who can project my visions."

She dialed what he had to assume was her friend's number but a moment later looked defeated, saying it had gone to voice mail.

Kirin tugged her back into his lap. "It's the middle of the night. She'll call you back. This will help if we can prove your innocence, and then we can freely move around to figure out what Gideon is really after."

Talia nodded.

"You're sleepy, my mate."

She nodded and yawned. "Let's go to bed."

Kirin stood with Talia in his arms. It felt good to have her close. His dragon seemed settled. Normally, his dragon only seemed to settle after a fight or in his home. He didn't like being away.

"You don't want to tuck her in and come back down? We could see which one of us can win the drinking game," Conley suggested.

Kirin laughed. "No. When you have a mate, you'll understand."

Conley shook his head. "I'm not ready for a mate. Too young. Too much to do before I settle down."

Kirin rolled his eyes. He could tell his brother didn't believe his own words. It would only be a matter of time before Conley found his mate. Since finding Talia, Kirin wanted his brothers to experience what he was experiencing.

"We'll see what your dragon has to say about that." Kirin had a feeling when Conley found his mate, he would fall just as hard as Kirin had and probably faster.

19

TALIA

Kirin carried Talia to bed. She was happier than she'd been in a really long time. And even though this should have been a scary time for her, she felt like she could face anything life threw at her because of Kirin.

"Sleepy?" he asked.

She shook her head. "Now that we're alone, really alone, what do you want to do?" She bit her cheek. "Can I meet your dragon again?"

Kirin glanced at the balcony. "We could go for a quick flight."

Talia followed Kirin over to the glass doors. She couldn't wait to see her mate's dragon again. Kirin opened the doors. The cold night didn't hinder her excitement. The sky was clear. She would get to see him fly.

"Okay, when I change, climb on to my back."

Talia let out a squeak. "I don't understand."

Kirin gave her a lopsided grin. "We are going for a flight."

"*We*, as in, I'm going with you? I'm not so sure about this. What happens if I fall?"

Kirin ran his knuckles down her face. "I will never let you fall."

"Okay."

Her okay was all Kirin must have needed. He started to discard his clothes. His sexy abs shone in the moonlight. His eyes had become pure gold with a black slit down the center. Most people would have been scared, but to Talia, his eyes were beautiful. Once his clothes were discarded, a shimmer appeared before her, and a second later, a twenty-foot dragon stood on the balcony.

"You're so pretty."

The large dragon huffed, causing Talia to pull back. *You can touch me.*

"Did I just hear you in my mind?"

Yes.

Talia slowly stepped forward and ran her hand across the gold scales, which shimmered in the moonlight. She thought he would feel hot to the touch, but he felt the same. She glanced at his back. It was high, and she had no clue how she would get up. *Would it be rude to ask him to wear a saddle?*

"YES, IT WOULD." Somehow, the huge dragon managed to roll his eyes. *Step back for a second.*

She couldn't help but jump at his command. Hearing Kirin in her mind would take some getting used to. When Talia gave him enough room, he lay across the balcony floor. Talia sucked in her breath and climbed up the back of the dragon. Then she leaned forward and wrapped her arms around his neck.

Kirin leaped off the balcony. No warning, nothing—he jumped into the night, and it felt like they were free-falling. Talia was pretty sure she let out a scream on the way down before Kirin stretched his wings and took them back up into the night sky. The air breezed past them. He soared down the mountain before heading straight back up. She could feel his powerful wings working to keep them high in the sky. When they were close to the local river, he swooped back down, and she could see her reflection.

The image would be in her mind forever. *Too bad no one could take a picture of me riding Kirin.* Kirin jerked to the left and headed upward. "Where are we going?"

Somewhere special to me and my dragon.

Talia didn't need to ask any more questions to know they were going to where he hid his hoard. She tightened her arms around his neck and enjoyed the view below as they went toward Kirin's secret lair. Kirin swooped down to a ledge on the side of the mountain. They had flown for a good twenty minutes. When he stopped, Talia crawled off his back and looked over the edge. That was the wrong thing to do. She hadn't realized how far up Kirin had taken her.

Strong arms grabbed her from behind. "Come on. I want to show you something."

Talia turned to follow Kirin. "Where did you find clothes?" She was so busy looking over the cliff at the potentially deathly drop that she hadn't seen Kirin get dressed.

"I keep a spare set up here. Now, do you want to really know where I hide my clothing, or do you want to see my lair?"

Talia followed closely behind Kirin as he walked

up the mountainside. She couldn't see any entrance. "You sure we're in the right place?"

Kirin gave her a lopsided grin. "Yes. One second." As Kia had done earlier, he placed his hand on the wall, and the rocks started to move. Kirin tugged her into the mountain opening, and rocks closed behind them. What he did next was amazing—he blew fire into a gold pot in the center of the room, and his fire moved along a gold trough that lined the ceiling. The place was lit with Kirin's fire.

"This place is amazing. You built this yourself?"

Kirin pulled her into his arms and kissed her lips. He pulled away too quickly. "No. I hired some of Kia's builders and few witches."

"Aren't you worried they'll come back and take your things?" Talia glanced around the main room, though the word *room* didn't do the place justice. It had to be five thousand square feet. Mounds of gold and jewels lay across the floor. They sparkled under the light of Kirin's fire.

"No. Anything to do with my lair was erased from all the workers' minds." When Talia scowled, he said, "Don't worry. Each person knew what they were getting into before they were hired. Now, come with me so I can show you my favorite part."

Talia followed Kirin to the back of the massive room, where he opened a large oak door. Behind it was a large bed. The room was illuminated with Kirin's fire.

"Kirin, this place is amazing. Is this where you live and sleep?"

Her mate let out a chuckle. "No, this is where I store my hoard, and every so often, my dragon likes to stay here for a few days. Hence the huge bed."

"You sleep in here as your dragon?"

Kirin pulled her into his arms. "Do you want to spend the night talking about my dragon's sleeping habits, or do you want to explore the bed? I personally want to explore your body and bring you to pleasure."

Her mate didn't wait for her response. He started to unbutton his pants. She couldn't pull her eyes away from his hands as he worked his pants down. She loved him. She couldn't wait to wrap her legs around him again. The last time, her mate had spent hours worshipping her body.

Wanting to show him how much she loved him, Talia dropped to her knees in front of Kirin. She tilted her head back to see her mate. His eyes flashed between brown and gold. Both man and dragon needed her. His cock strained to be released.

She slowly slid his boxers down and gently ran

her hands up his thighs. His muscles twitched under her hand. She couldn't believe how strong he was. The other night, he'd picked her up and carried her to bed like she weighed nothing.

Talia wanted to see the fire in Kirin's eyes. She slowly raised her shirt off over her head. She was wearing a white lace bra. Kirin's breath hitched as she threw her shirt to the side. She had never been that forward before. She never used to freely undress with lights on. But being around Kirin made her overcome some of her insecurities.

Talia shyly looked up at her mate, and she realized he didn't see any of her flaws, or maybe he liked her more for the flaws she had. The lust in his eyes made her want to please her mate more.

"Beautiful mate," Kirin groaned as she wrapped her lips around his member.

Talia cupped his balls and continued to work his shaft in her mouth. When she looked up, Kirin's eyes locked on her every movement. His hands fisted at his sides, trying to hold control. Talia released her hands from his cock and reached back to undo the white lace bra as she continued to bob her head.

The view must have been too much for her mate. Her stomach clenched at the way his hands held her, taking control of the pace. By the moans Kirin was making, she knew he was close, and she wanted him to come. Talia reached around, clenched Kirin's ass, and pulled him deeper into her mouth.

The dick in her mouth seemed to get harder with each pass she made. Talia wanted her mate to come, but one moment she was on her knees in front of him, and the next, she was flat on her back, looking up at the most gorgeous gold eyes. His mouth was on her before she could ask what had happened.

He devoured her, and she loved every second of it. Kirin worked the buttons of her jeans as his tongue swept her mouth. Every sense in her body was on fire. She couldn't get enough of her mate. Kirin reached down to help push her jeans off. They'd barely hit the floor when his hands spread her legs.

Kirin ran a finger along her slit. With each touch, her body burned more for him to be inside of her, and she couldn't wait for the feeling of them being together. "I need you," she said, pressing her hips up for more friction against his hand.

"I want a taste first," Kirin ground out as he worked kisses down her body and captured her areola in his mouth.

"Please, Kirin. I need you in me."

Kirin most have saw something in her eyes,

because he shoved her legs farther apart, leaned down, and kissed the side of her neck. She could feel his member sliding against her slit. She reached down, not waiting for him to push in. His cock twitched under her hand, making her clit tingle with anticipation.

Her mate pressed inside her slowly, and she tried to raise her hips to get him to go deeper. Kirin smiled down at her. "I want to enjoy every second, my beautiful mate."

"I need more," she pleaded.

Kirin leaned down and locked his lips around her nipple and sucked hard. The pleasure was coming from everywhere. The wave of her orgasm came hard and strong, her body arching into his. Her fingers trembled as she gripped his biceps until her body no longer felt like it was floating.

Within seconds, Kirin started to breathe heavily as his hips moved faster, pumping his dick in and out of her quick and hard. Talia threw her head back on the pillow and was lost in the feeling of her mate.

His jaw clenched, and he looked intent, a sheen of sweat forming on his brow. "I'm coming," he growled between thrusts, and with one final push, he buried himself inside of her.

Talia and Kirin both lay in the bed with gold

surrounding them, panting, still connected as they recovered. Kirin slowly pulled out and turned to his side, pulling Talia into his arms.

"Wow," Talia whispered.

Kirin ran his hands down Talia's side. "I love you, my sweet mate."

Talia's breath hitched. "I don't know how it's possible, but I love you. It's strange. I know we just met, but my mind and body are consumed by you. I never thought I would trust anyone as much as I trust you." She turned in Kirin's arms and leaned forward to kiss her mate. "I love you, Kirin."

"We need to head back," Kirin said.

On the way out of the cave, Talia flicked a gold coin into a fountain and wished they would clear her and Alida's names soon.

20

KIRIN

The morning sun shone through the floor-length windows. Kirin had not slept since they returned from showing Talia his hoard. The council coming after Alida and Talia had unsettled his dragon. She stirred in his arms. Her smile astounded him, and he could not believe how lucky he was to have found the perfect mate.

Talia's phone shrieked on the nightstand, breaking the silence. She reached over and grabbed it. He caught a glimpse of the name that flashed across the screen. *Nyx.* This was the call that could help prove Alida and Talia's innocence.

Talia swiped her finger across the iPhone screen. "Nyx."

The sadness and worry in Talia's voice made his

dragon rumble. Talia glanced in his direction with a raised brow. He didn't have time to explain his inner dragon's need to protect. Instead, he leaned forward and placed a kiss on her forehead.

"Nyx, I need your help, but you need to understand that helping me might put you in danger." Talia paused for a second and squeezed her eyes closed. "I'm currently running from the council."

With his sensitive hearing, Kirin could hear Nyx on the other end of the line.

"It's been a while since I caused any real drama. I'm down."

"Are you sure?" Talia said. "You can get in trouble."

Kirin had never met Nyx in person before. However, he could imagine her rolling her eyes. "Yes, I want to help. I know you would do the same thing for me."

"Okay. Remember that park we would go to as kids?"

"Yes."

"Meet me there in two hours." Talia ended the call.

"Why are we not having Alida transport us there?" Kirin asked.

Talia licked her lips. "We will need her to get us

all into the council warehouse later. If she is going to transport us all in, she will need all of her energy."

Kirin pulled Talia into his arms and pressed his lips to hers. She was like a drug to him—he couldn't get enough of her. He deepened the kiss, and Talia melted into his arms. Fire coursed through his body. The need to possess her was strong. The world faded away. He knew in the back of his mind that he needed to stop the kiss before it continued much longer. When he pulled away, Talia's pupils were dilated with hunger.

She was leaning into him when a loud bang came against the bedroom door. She jumped out of his arms, and the door sprang open. Kirin reached over and pulled her back to his side while Kia leaned against the doorjamb with a cocky smirk.

"Did your friend call?"

Kirin flung a pillow at his brother. "Go away."

Talia pulled at his arms. "We need to get going. I told Nyx we would be there in two hours."

Kirin knew Talia was right, but he still flipped his brother off for intruding on their private moment. Kia chuckled as he closed the door. Kirin tried to pull Talia back into his arms, but she slipped away.

"We need to get going. When we clear Alida's name, we can pick back up where we left off."

He didn't like not having his mate in his arms. Kirin reluctantly rolled to the side and grabbed his jeans from the night before. When he stood to find a shirt, he caught his mate staring at him. She licked her juicy lips.

"If you keep looking at me like that, we will never meet your friend on time." Talia ducked her head and pulled on her clothes from the day before.

Once they finished dressing, they headed toward the kitchen. Kirin smiled at the sound of Alida laughing at one of his brother's dumb jokes. When they rounded the corner, Alida smiled and jumped off the chair and ran to Talia's side. Talia blinked a couple of times to hold her emotions.

"About time you both got up," the little girl lectured, her hands on her hips.

Kirin bent down and picked her up. "The sun hasn't even risen completely. When did you get up?"

"Grandma Judy made pancakes, and I smelled them."

Kirin looked at his mom. She had the brightest smile. Like Talia, Judy blinked back tears. Deep down, Kirin knew Alida would bring big things to his new family. He put her back in the chair she'd climbed out of and took the seat next to her. "Alida."

When the little girl looked up at him, she had a

sad smile. "Don't worry, Kirin. I won't ever forget my real mom and dad. They will always be in my heart." She pressed her little hand to her heart. "Mom taught me so many things, but she said I can't keep being sad. It's hard not being sad, but Mom said I need to be strong so we can clear my name."

"How did you know what I wanted to talk about? And when did you talk to your mom?" Kirin looked over Alida's head at his mate. Talia had tears streaming down her face. Judy had her arm wrapped around Talia's waist. His two brothers stood still, watching the little girl.

Alida reached forward and took his hand. "You're worried I'm not coping with my parents' deaths. Mom came to me the first night. She told me Talia and you would be my future. You both would take care of me and make sure I was safe." Alida's lip quivered. "I told her I didn't want her to go, but she said it was her time and she and Dad would always look over me."

Talia rushed to Alida's side. "We will figure out who did this to your parents. Then I want to hear everything about your mom. Kirin and I will make sure your parents' memories live on. And we understand if you are sad, you don't need to hide your feelings."

Alida wrapped her little arms around Talia's neck. "Okay." Talia pulled back and took the chair on the other side of Alida.

Kirin grabbed a pancake off the stack. "So the plan today is to project Talia's vision to the council. Nyx is on board. We need to meet her in an hour. From there, we drive to the council warehouse, and Alida will transport us inside. I plan to call Kael when we are close so he can gather everyone."

Talia glanced down at Alida. "Maybe Alida should stay here with Judy, and we can go confront the council."

The air in the room turned cold. Talia's teeth chattered. Even for Kirin, the temperature felt off.

"No!" Alida screamed. "I need to go."

Kirin squeezed her shoulder. "Alida, you can come. Talia's just worried. But you need to stop what you are doing." The girl's powers were getting out of control. They would need to figure out what to do once they cleared her name.

Alida glanced at Talia and closed her eyes. "Sorry," she whispered. The temperature in the room came back to normal.

Kirin glanced up at the clock. "We need to head out." Everyone piled into Kia's Navigator. Kia took the driver's seat, and Kirin sat next to him. Alida and

Talia sat in the middle, and Conley sat in the back with his mom.

Kirin watched out the window as they drove down the mountain. Kia picked the winding back road through the unclaimed territory. Kirin hoped the vast mountain would always stay unclaimed.

Alida giggled in the back seat. Kirin turned and winked at his mate, but he saw a wolf in another vehicle that sent a shiver down his back. Before he could tell Kia something was off, Kia slammed the brakes of the SUV. The vehicle fishtailed as it came to a stop.

"Stay in the car." Kirin jumped out of the SUV. Jeremiah and two wolves Kirin did not recognize exited the SUV that cut them off. He heard additional footsteps behind him. When he glanced back from the SUV, two more men stood outside the Navigator. Kirin chanted for his dragon, but nothing happened. He looked at Kia, who looked as shocked as he felt.

Anger flooded his veins when he heard Talia scream. Kirin turned his hatred toward Jeremiah. "What do you want?"

"We've come for the girls. We don't care about you or your brothers," Jeremiah said in an even tone, but Kirin could tell he was nervous. Even though he couldn't uses his powers, that didn't stop him from seeing the sweat dribble down the side of Jeremiah's face.

Kirin stepped closer, the gravel road crunching under his boats. "Do you really think your men will win this fight? Even if you could take Alida and Talia today, we would hunt you down and kill you." Kirin looked at the nine men. "Where's Carter?"

Jeremiah laughed. "Carter is a weak alpha, and we found a new leader. Hail Gideon."

"Hail Gideon," four other men shouted, each one dressed in full tactical gear. Jeremiah was the only one with his face showing.

Kirin had only met Jeremiah a few times over the years. He did a shitty job of bringing people in, but betraying his alpha didn't sound like him. But Kirin found that the loss of his dragon bothered him more than anything else.

"Did you really think five men would be enough to go against the last immortal dragons?"

All five men looked utterly stunned, glancing at Kirin and back at Jeremiah.

"Hey, you said they were human—nothing about them being dragons," the man to Jeremiah's left squeaked.

"Don't worry. They can't use their powers," Jeremiah said in a cocky tone. "Now, get the girl."

Kirin turned his focus from Jeremiah to the man who held Alida. The young girl squirmed in the hired guns' arms. She had tears running down her face. Kirin's only thought was rescuing Alida and Talia.

"Make what's messing with my dragon stop."

"Let's kick some dog ass, brother." Kia turned toward Jeremiah.

Conley was fighting two hired guns behind the SUV. Judy lay on the ground, blood running from her head. A man had his hands on Talia, but she fought hard. Choosing between his mate and Alida tore Kirin apart.

"ALIDA!" Talia screamed. Kirin looked at her one more time before he went after the man holding the girl. Talia would know that it devastated him that he had to leave her to fend for herself.

Talia scraped at the man's hand wrapped around her arm. Leaning in, she bit it. He shoved her forward against the SUV. "Fucking bitch. Get back here."

The hired gun lunged in her direction. She waited until the last second before she moved to the side. When he ran into the SUV, she punched the mercenary in the side with all her strength. Talia wasn't sure what she should aim for, but she'd seen when people were hit hard on the side, it hurt. She must have hit the right side, because man doubled over and dropped to the ground.

Talia looked up and saw the mercenary with Alida in his arms, holding a gun pointed at Kirin. Kirin didn't seem to even notice the gun. His eyes were trained on the mercenary's eyes, his muscles tensed.

Talia ran toward the man pointing a gun at her mate and the child she loved. With two steps closer to her family, she heard footsteps behind her before a pain she had never felt before hit her back. As she screamed and fell to the gravel, a gunshot was fired through the air.

Everything happened so fast. Tires skidded to a stop near the SUV, Kirin grunted before a second shot was fired, and Talia felt another horrific sharp pain as a knee went into her back. She gasped for air as the girl she cared for screamed bloody murder. The last thing Talia heard was Alida's scream for help. Then Talia felt the hit to the back of her head.

21

KIRIN

Alida's scream echoed through Kirin's head. He'd let his mate down as well as a young girl who depended on him. Kirin's last hope was to demand information on where Jeremiah planned to take Alida. There was no way Gideon would bring the young girl to the council warehouse. Kirin didn't worry about Jeremiah's five goons—Kia held both of them off.

Kirin squeezed Jeremiah's neck. In the back of his mind, he knew he had to loosen his grip. "Where did you take them?"

Jeremiah scraped at Kirin's hands. "Kirin, you need to let up. He is the only hope of finding Alida." Kirin loosened his grip around the man's throat, not seeing the Taser in Jeremiah's hand until it was too late. Kirin dropped his grip, and Jeremiah took off running, but he didn't get too far—Kirin was reaching to pull him back when a lightning bolt rang down from the sky. His only hope for finding Alida dropped to the ground.

Kirin quickly pressed his fingers to Jeremiah's neck. He could feel the pulse. Kirin looked around for the warlocks. He'd recognized the lightning bolt. The two men Kia had fought with also lay on the ground. Kia looked at him, confused. Talia's lifeless body lay next to his mother's. Conley crouched beside them, a sheen of tears in his eyes.

"Show yourself."

The two warlocks walked in from the side of the road. "Is that any way to talk to the man who stopped everyone?"

Kirin took two steps toward the warlock. "You ruined any chance of getting my girl back."

Alatar, the older of the two warlocks, rolled his eyes. "For being so old, you are very dramatic."

"I will show you dram—" Kirin's words were cut off as another SUV barreled toward them. Talia groaned on the ground. Kirin's dragon was still dormant. When the SUV had barely come to a stop, the passenger's-side door flew open. Alida jumped out and ran to Talia. Kirin had to blink. When he zeroed in on the driver's-side window, Talia's neighbor stepped out of the car.

With no time to figure out what was going on, he rushed to Talia's side. She sat up and wrapped her arms around Alida. "Are you okay, sweet girl?"

"Yeah, Ms. Bethlow saved me. She was so cool."

Talia looked off from the little girl to her neighbor, who stood next to the two wizards. "Ms. Bethlow?"

"Hello, my dear. You look like you went ten rounds." The old lady turned to the two warlocks. "Well, you'd better go gather the douchebags." Kirin didn't know what surprised him more—the warlocks being there, or the fact that they did what the older lady told them without blinking.

"Thank you," Talia whispered.

Ms. Bethlow waved her hand. "No thank-you needed. You three will do great things. Now, don't you have a little girl's name to clear? Don't worry about these men. We'll take care of it."

"I don't understand," Kirin said.

She winked at him. "I will explain everything in due time. Let me go make sure my boys don't mess anything up."

"What is she?" Kirin asked Talia when the elder lady was out of ear's reach.

"I thought she was human... but we need to get to Nyx."

Kirin looked over to Conley, who held his mom. The mercenaries had shot Judy with a tranquilizer. "Alida, I need you to do something. I know you won't want to, but we need your help."

The little girl's lip quivered as she nodded.

"I need you to take Judy and Conley back to Kia's house." Alida started to shake her head. "Precious, they hurt my mom, and she can't continue. I need you to help my mom."

Alida glanced at Judy and gave Talia a hug before she climbed off Talia's lap. "I can't. My powers don't work."

Ms. Bethlow shouted from a few feet away. "Walk thirty feet that way, and they will work. That is how Jyna and Alatar used their magic."

Conley stood with Judy in his arms, and Alida followed. When they got to the trees, Alida reached for Conley's hand, and they vanished.

No longer worrying about Alida, Kirin turned back to Talia, "Are you sure you feel up to this?"

"Yes."

Kirin reached down and picked Talia up.

"What are you doing?" she asked. "I can walk."

"I know, but I need this."

Ms. Bethlow smiled in their direction. Kia jumped into the driver's seat. Kirin watched in the review mirror as the warlocks and Ms. Bethlow pushed Jeremiah's men into the back of the SUV. A few car lengths away from the scene, Kia swerved, and Kirin hunched over at the same time. Both of their dragons were no longer dormant. Kirin's talons extended. He didn't need to look in the front to know his brother's dragon was near as well. The suppression of their dragons pissed them both off, but their dragons would crush the car if they changed inside of the SUV.

When Talia rested her hand on his shoulder, Kirin closed his eyes and took a few more deep breaths. His inner beast settled. Kia, on the other hand, was struggling.

"Come on, Kia. We need to prove Alida's innocence. I promise we can burn those fuckers later." With each word he spoke, his brother's dragon simmered down. "Now, let's go prove my girl innocent, and our dragons can have snack later."

Kia nodded and wrapped his fingers around the steering wheel. They were running late to meet Nyx, and Kirin hoped she would still be at the park when they arrived. When Kia rounded the last corner, a yellow Volkswagen bug was sitting parked at the far end of the lot. A woman in high black boots and long black hair sat on the hood, looking at her phone.

"That's her," Talia told Kia.

The car came to a stop next to Nyx. Talia jumped out, threw her arms around her friend, and tugged her into the car. Now they had the key to clearing Talia and Alida's names.

"Not trying to be rude, Talia, but you look like shit." Nyx laughed.

Talia huffed in the back seat. "Well, we were just attacked by mercenaries."

Nyx sobered up. "Is everyone okay?"

"Yes, you need to understand that Gideon is out for blood."

Nyx tugged her sweatshirt. "I'm here for you. Let's do this."

When they were two miles away from the ware-house, Kirin pulled out his cell phone and called Kael, who answered on the third ring. "This isn't a good time."

"I don't care what's going on. A bunch of mercenaries attacked us, and they stopped my dragon. We are on our way to the warehouse now. We have proof Alida didn't kill her parents."

Kael let out a sigh. "Okay. What do you need from me?"

"Gather as many council members as you can to meet us outside. We'll be there in a few." Kirin didn't wait for Kael to respond. He hung up and grabbed his mate's hand.

For the last couple of miles, the air in the SUV was heavy. Kirin could see a group gathered outside the warehouse when they got there. He sent a silent thank-you to Kael. If he had to use his dragon and save his mate, it would be easier outside than inside the building. Gideon wouldn't be able to use whatever device he had with other high-ranking councilmen around. There was no way would they allow their powers to be dormant.

"Ready to become a free woman?" Kirin asked Talia as he gripped her hand. They stepped out of the vehicle, and council guards rushed toward them.

Kirin's dragon started to emerge. "Stop." Everyone froze in place. "Talia, tell the council what you found out."

Talia stepped forward. Kirin could see pure hatred in Gideon's eyes. "Well, let's hear what you have to say before they sentence you."

Kirin couldn't hold back the rumble from his dragon. Talia rested a hand on his shoulder. "Over the past two days, I've looked into Alida's c—"

Gideon took another menacing step forward. "We don't pay you to look into the case. We pay you for visions, and you saw nothing." The growing number of council members started to talk to each other.

Kael stepped next to Gideon. "Tell us your vision, Talia, or we will have to arrest you."

"I was trying to until Gideon interrupted," she said. Gideon's eyes flashed a deep red. "I went back to Alida's house and touched items to get a better vision of what happened. The knife didn't give me enough information. The vision on it seemed to have been tampered with." The crowd started to rumble with questions. Talia waited for them to quiet down before she continued. "My original assessment that someone tampered with the knife was correct. When I went to the crime scene and touched Maya's blood, I saw someone attack Maya and Jalil. The girl didn't do it, and the person was erased from the vision."

"If you were so sure about the altered vision, why did you run?" Gideon countered.

"I didn't try to run. I wanted to see what Alida's

vision was. I wanted to compare, but when I touched her, her powers kicked in, and we teleported. We ended up at her house. And there, I saw more."

Gideon shifted slightly. "Very convenient. Too bad no one else can see."

Nyx stepped forward. "I can help." She pushed back the hood on her shirt. Gideon started to open his mouth, but she reached out and touched Talia before he could say anything. The vision that played against the warehouse was what Talia had seen when she touched Maya's blood. Maya and Jalil were talking to an invisible figure. The council members gasped when the invisible person snapped Jalil's neck and then Maya's. Someone in the crowd demanded that she stop showing the vision. Talia and Nyx ignored the pleas and continued to play the vision. Kirin went back and forth between watching the show and looking at Talia. She had tears streaming down her face. The crowd could only see the vision, but he knew his mate was reliving the agony. Finally, the last part of the vision played out as the mystery person used his or her magic to stab the dead bodies.

Talia closed her eyes and pulled her hand from Nyx. She leaned against Kirin. He could tell the vision had drained her.

Kael stepped next to Gideon. "I'm convinced Alida didn't kill her parents. We need to figure out who is manipulating these visions and how."

"How are we not sure Talia didn't manipulate the vision?" Gideon asked.

The council members mumbled. Voices started to rise as the people argued with each other. Savannah, a long-time council member, silenced the crowd. "Talia has worked for us for years. I think we should let her go and figure out who is manipulating the vision."

"If this is the case, then you're all in grave danger, wouldn't you think?" Gideon had a glint in his eye. For the first time, Kirin actually believed that something might be going on with Gideon, although he wasn't sure how he could prove it. "Maybe we should hold the girl and Talia until we know they didn't do it."

Savannah let her power flow. "This is a young girl you are talking about. All council members are here, so let's put it to a vote. Who thinks we should let Talia and the girl go?"

Kirin's dragon paced at the thought of his mate being taken into custody. When none of the members spoke of freeing Talia, she mumbled, "Assholes."

Kael was the first member of the council to raise his hand. "They should go free." Then each member, except Gideon, nodded in agreement. "Looks like you're free to go," Kael announced.

There was one more thing they needed to resolve before they left. "Talia and I would like to adopt Alida," Kirin said.

"No," Gideon shouted.

Savannah's voice rose over the crowd. "I've reviewed Maya and Jalil's will, and it states that Kael has the choice of where Alida would go if anything should happen to them."

"That can't be right. I was Jalil's closest friend," Gideon said. Kirin took that bit of information and stored it away.

"Alida needs a home with two people who will love her. Talia, you risked your life to protect the girl. I will grant you temporary custody of Alida. I want to speak to her before I grant you full rights. Kirin, looking at the way you and Talia are acting, I assume you mated. I can't think of a better home for her. Now, I believe the council has some work ahead of us."

Everyone shuffled back inside, but Gideon waited until they were out of hearing range. Then he walked over to where Kirin stood with Talia. Kirin saw Kael, not inside yet, stop to watch.

"Do you think you really won?" Gideon asked before he turned and headed back toward the warehouse.

EPILOGUE - TALIA

"Talia, I think you've decorated enough," Kirin said.

"I want it to be perfect."

"The piece of paper in the frame makes it perfect. All of this"—Kirin waved his arms around the living room of his house—"is a little overboard. I love you, my mate, but our daughter only needs a little party to celebrate." His voice softened when tears formed in Talia's eyes. "Don't cry, my mate. She will love it, but you seem tired, and you keep pushing yourself. We need you to go to the doctor and find out what's wrong."

"I made an appointment for tomorrow afternoon. Everything for Alida's party needs to be perfect. The witch doctor told me tomorrow would be just fine. When I explained what was wrong, she said she had an idea but wanted to see me in person first."

They were standing in the living room of her and Kirin's house. The three of them had stayed with Kia for a couple of days after clearing their names. When it seemed Gideon wasn't going to bother them anymore, they moved into Kirin's house. Talia and Alida spent the first weekend redoing the spare bedroom into Alida's pink palace. Alida had wormed herself deep into Talia's heart. Talia wanted to give the young girl the world.

Talia talked to Ms. Bethlow when they went to gather more of her clothes. She was the mother of the three warlocks. She'd told her boys to take Jeremiah and the others back to Virginia, and any information they discovered, they would let her know. Ms. Bethlow didn't believe that her middle child was dead. Gideon had him, and she wanted her son back.

Kirin came up behind Talia and wrapped his arms around her waist. "What made you frown?"

She leaned back into her mate's arms. The world felt like a safe place when she was in his arms. She didn't want to taint the day by bringing up Gideon. "Do you think she is going to like the party?"

"Of course. She might only be eight years old, but she is as mature as an adult. I think part of it is her powers. Most kids would've broken down, but our girl did an amazing job. She has seen a psychiatrist each day. We will keep that up as long as it's needed."

Talia reached for another bag of party favors to set around the table. "Okay. What are Kia and Conley doing?"

Kirin let out a deep chuckle. "Kia bought her a state-of-the-art car, and now they are getting it ready."

She spun out of her mate's arms and placed her hands on her hips. "She's only eight. We are not letting them give her a car, Kirin."

Kirin gave her a lopsided smile she could never say no to. "It's an electric car. It shouldn't go too fast."

Talia already had to worry about her new daughter disappearing at any second, and now she had to worry about her in a car as well, even if it was a toy car. Footsteps on the marble floor made her turn to see who was there. Alida came running into the living and stopped when she noticed the pink décor.

Kirin walked over and grabbed her hand. "Hey, my sweet girl. You and Grandma are home early."

"I wanted to come home and talk to my new sister more."

Kirin looked at Talia with a confused look. "What are you talking about?"

Alida walked over to Talia and rested her hand on her belly. "My little sister. She talked to me yesterday."

Talia's hands went to her belly. "I can't be pregnant." *Well, I could, but how could Alida talk to a barely formed baby in my belly?* Talia looked up at Kirin.

He smiled at her and pulled her into his arms. "My beautiful mate," Kirin mumbled.

"Is this party for me?"

The young girl didn't realize what kind of bomb she'd dropped on her parents. Talia would have to take a test later. However, she already knew Alida had told her the truth.

"Yes, Alida," Kirin said. "The party is for you, but we weren't done setting it up. Talia and I also wanted to ask you a question."

"Yes."

"Don't you want to know what we are going to ask first?"

The girl rolled her eyes. "You are going to ask if I want to be your daughter. Yes, my mom said you would love and protect me, and I already like my new sister."

Talia bent down and pulled Alida into a hug.

"Looks like it's time to party!" Conley shouted from the doorway.

The rest of the afternoon was full of laughter and smiles. Talia couldn't believe how lucky she was for having found this family. She wished Conley and Kia could experience the happiness she and Kirin had. Talia would make it her next mission to make her new brothers-in-law happy.

The End!

Click here to pre-order The Dragon's Human

AUTHOR NOTE'S

White Hat Security Series

Hacker Exposed

Royal Hacker

Misunderstood Hacker

Undercover Hacker

Hacker Revelation

Hacker Christmas

Hacker Salvation

Nova Satellite Security Series
(White Hat Security Spin Off)

Pursuing Phoenix - Sept 3, 2019

Immortal Dragon

The Dragon's Psychic - July 9, 2019

The Dragon's Human - Sept 26, 2019

Montana Gold (Brotherhood Kindle World)

Grayson's Angel

Noah's Love

Bryson's Treasure - 2019

A Flipping Love Story (Badge of Honor World)

Unlocking Dreams

Unlocking Hope - 2019

Siblings of the Underworld

Hell's Key

Hell's Future - Aug 20, 2019

Visit linzibaxter.com for more information and release dates.
Join Linzi Baxter Newsletter at Newsletter

ABOUT AUTHOR

Linzi Baxter lives in Orlando, Florida with her husband and lazy basset hound. She started writing when voices inside her head wouldn't stop talking until the story was told. When not at work as an IT Manager, Linzi enjoys writing action-packed romances that will take you to the edge of your seat.

She enjoys engaging her readers with strong, interesting characters that have complex and stimulating stories to tell. If you enjoy a little (or maybe a whole lot) of steam and spice, don't miss checking out White Hat Security series.

When not writing, Linzi enjoys reading, watching college sports (GO UCF Knights), and traveling to Europe. She loves hearing from her readers and can't wait to hear from you!

Made in the USA
Monee, IL
29 January 2021